To Saturnino,
Evan, and Tyler
—A. M.

For my family.
I wouldn't want to be
tangled up with
anyone else.
—E. C.

SIMON & SCHUSTER BOOKS FOR YOUNG READERS
An imprint of Simon & Schuster Children's Publishing Division
1230 Avenue of the Americas, New York, New York 10020

Book design by Eric Comstock
The text for this book was set in Chennai Slab.
The illustrations for this book were rendered digitally.
Manufactured in China
0920 SCP
First Edition
10 9 8 7 6 5 4 3 2
CIP data for this book is available from the Library of Congress.
ISBN 978-1-4814-9721-3
ISBN 978-1-4814-9722-0 (eBook)

TANGLED

A story about shapes

written by
Anne Miranda

illustrated by
Eric Comstock

A PAULA WISEMAN BOOK
Simon & Schuster Books for Young Readers
New York London Toronto Sydney New Delhi

One day a little circle, just as happy as could be,

got caught inside a jungle gym and couldn't wiggle free.

Her friend, a tiny triangle, tried hard to get her out.

He tugged, but he got stuck as well, and both began to

A SQUARE

came on the double, climbing in to help them flee.

HE PUSHED AND PULLED

and twisted, but he couldn't set them free.

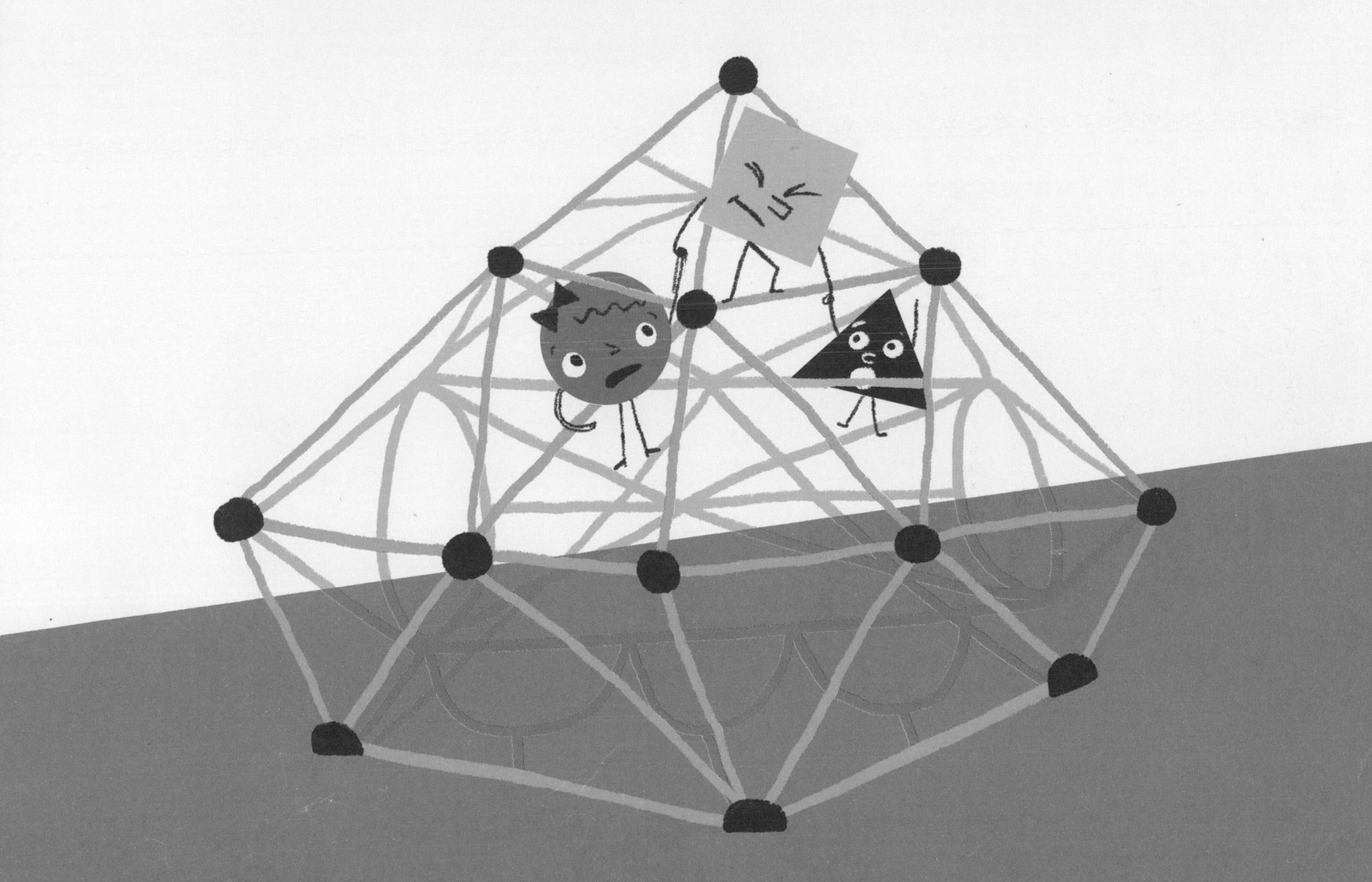

A rectangle ran over,
and he offered them a hand.

He tumbled

toward the jungle gym and
landed in the sand.

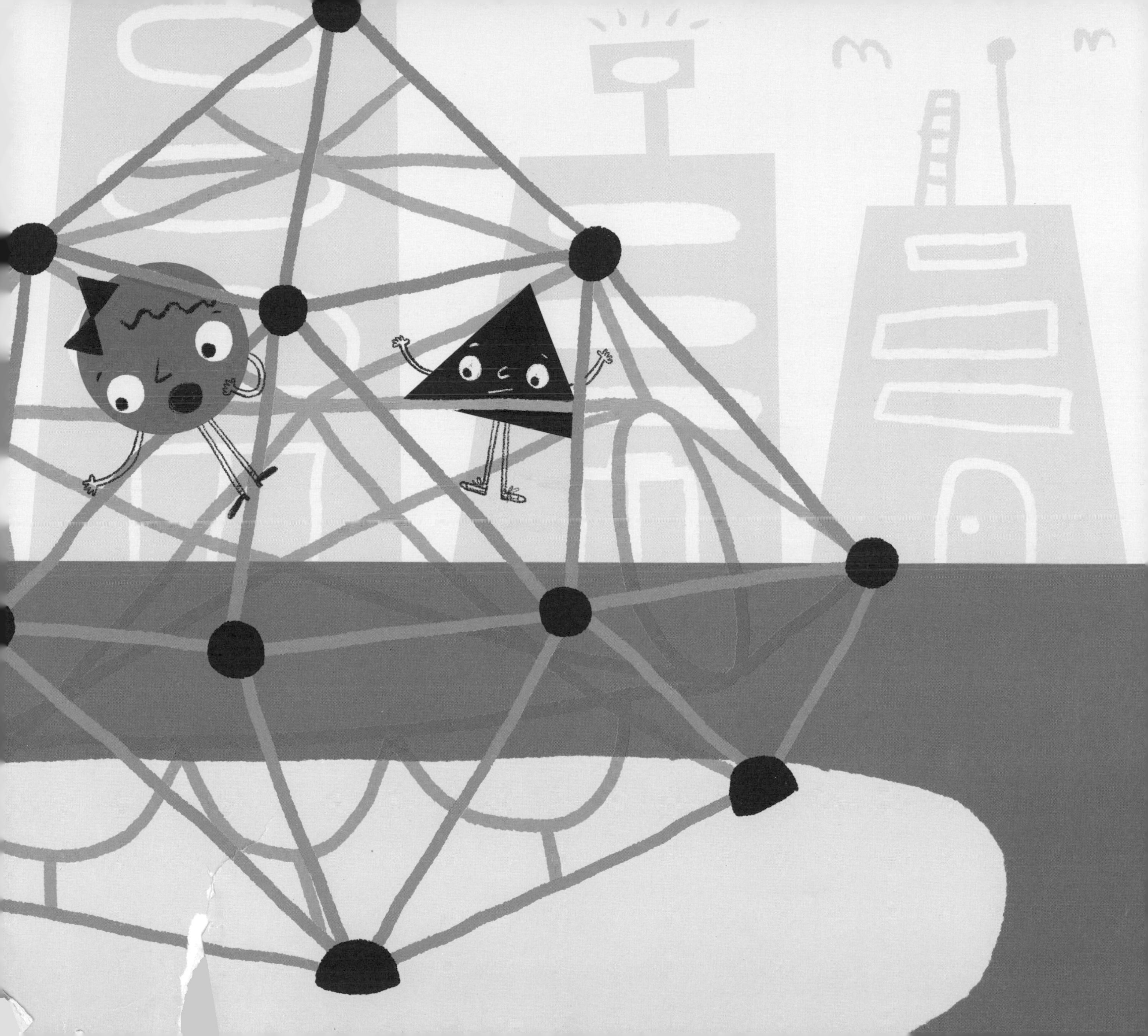

A slim ellipse who saw them
was the next to shimmy through.

But when he tried to get them out,

he got entangled too.

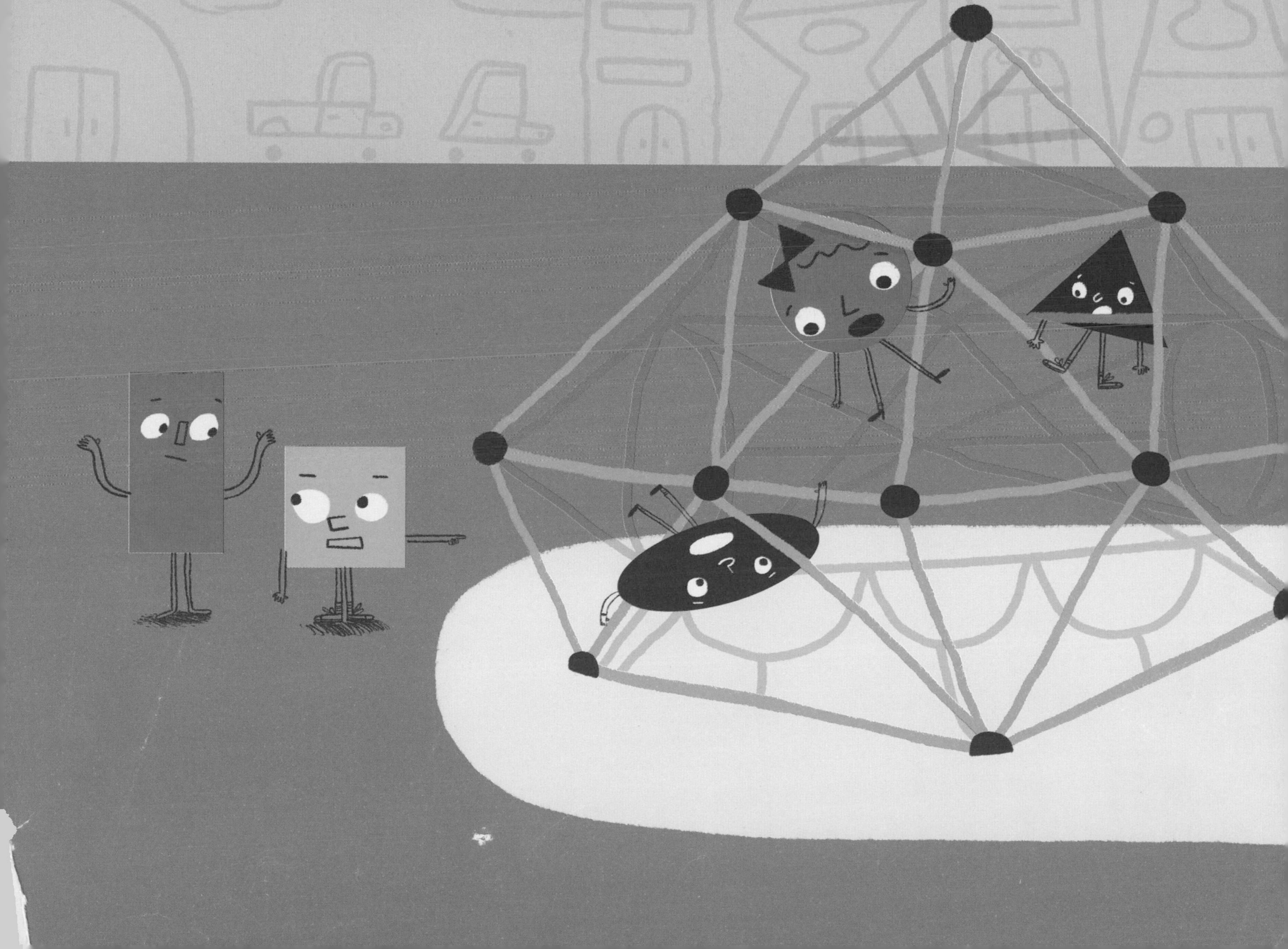

A cone directed traffic,
as the points began to flock.
The stars all congregated,
and the cubes went round the block.

The pentagon parade arrived
and did their very
BEST.

But every single one of them
was captured with the rest.

A trapezoid photographer took pictures of the scene.

A parallelogram felt sick and
turned
a little green.

What a HORROR!
What a MESS!

The shapes could not untwine.

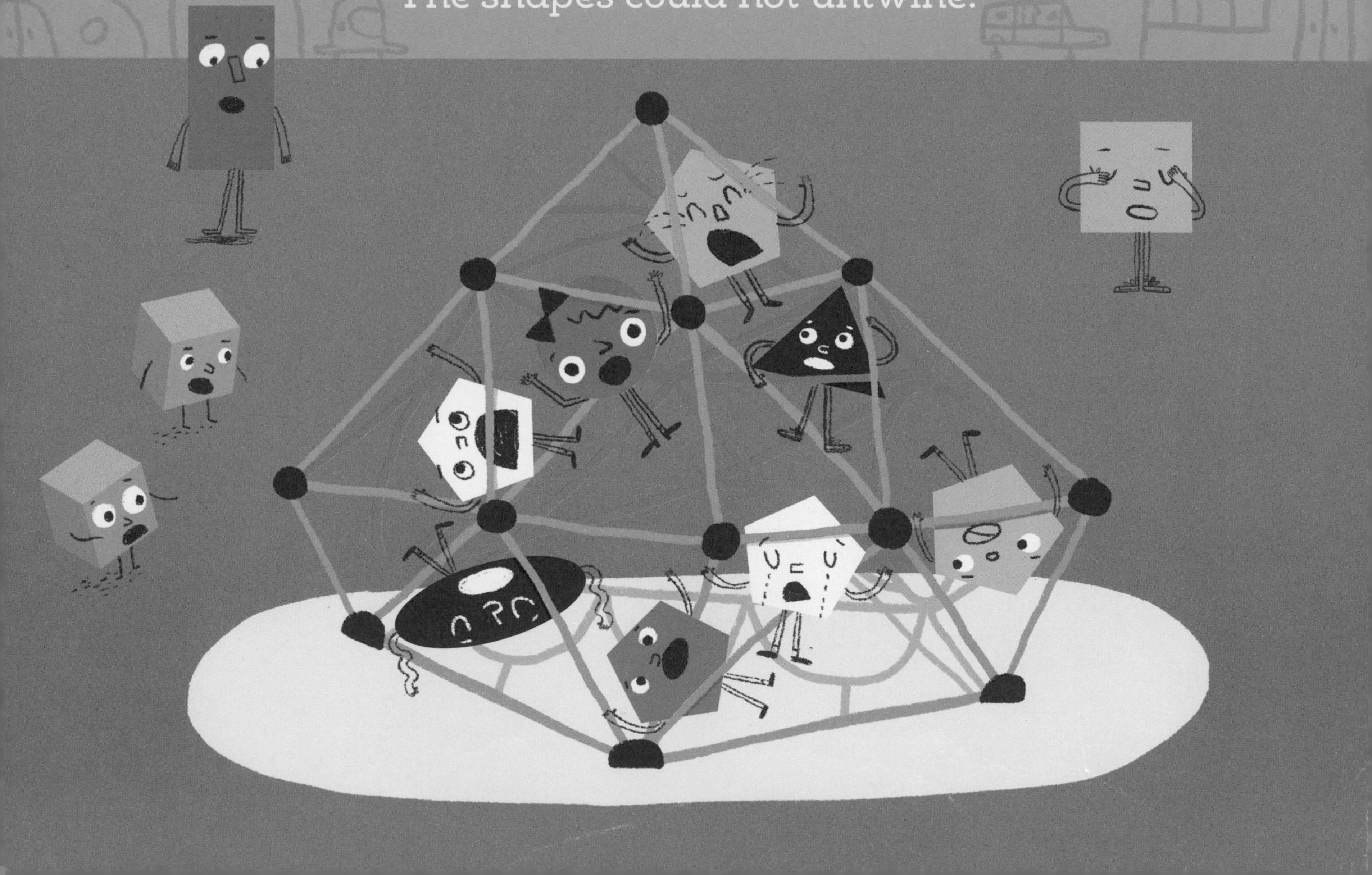

Then rushing to the rescue
came a straight and NARROW line.

SHE LOOKED

at every space and every curve

and every angle.

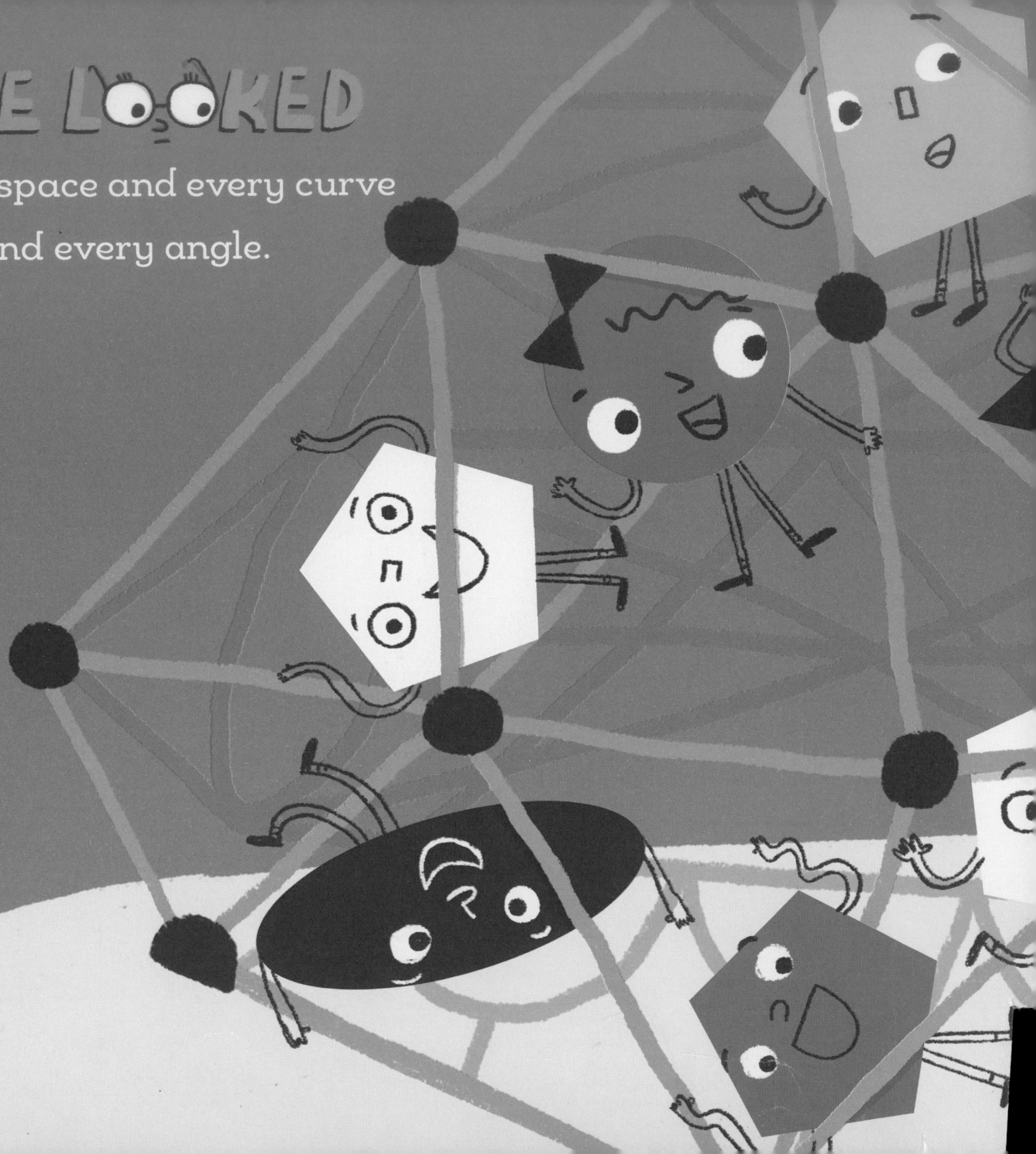

She had a clever plan
that would
undo the messy mangle.

She pleaded
with the other
SHAPES
for them to volunteer.

Out stepped a perfect prism
and a solid-looking sphere.

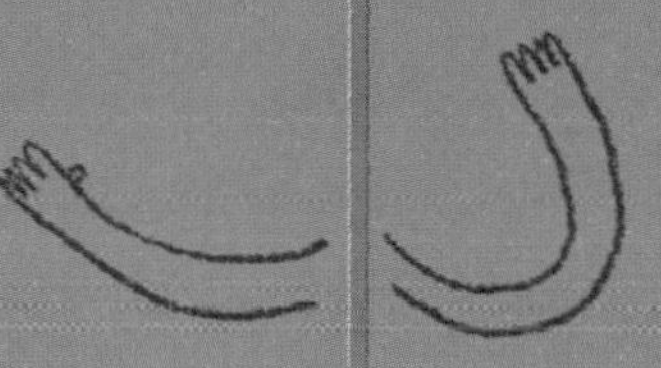

The plan was made...

THE SPHERE WOULD **JUMP**

upon the count of three.

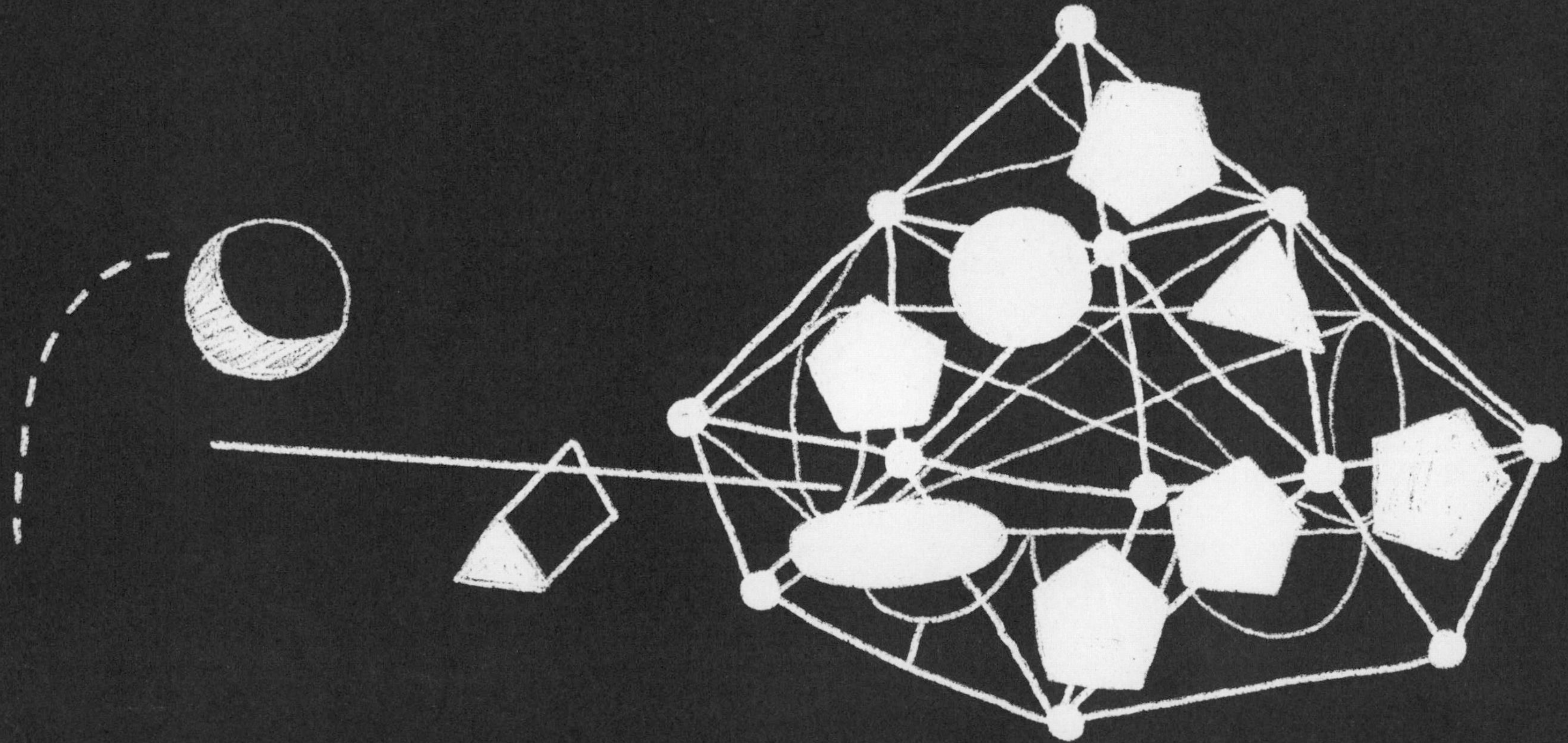

And polygons who heard the scheme
applauded it with glee.

EVERYBODY held their breath!
The sphere rolled up and hopped.
The prism and the line held tight,

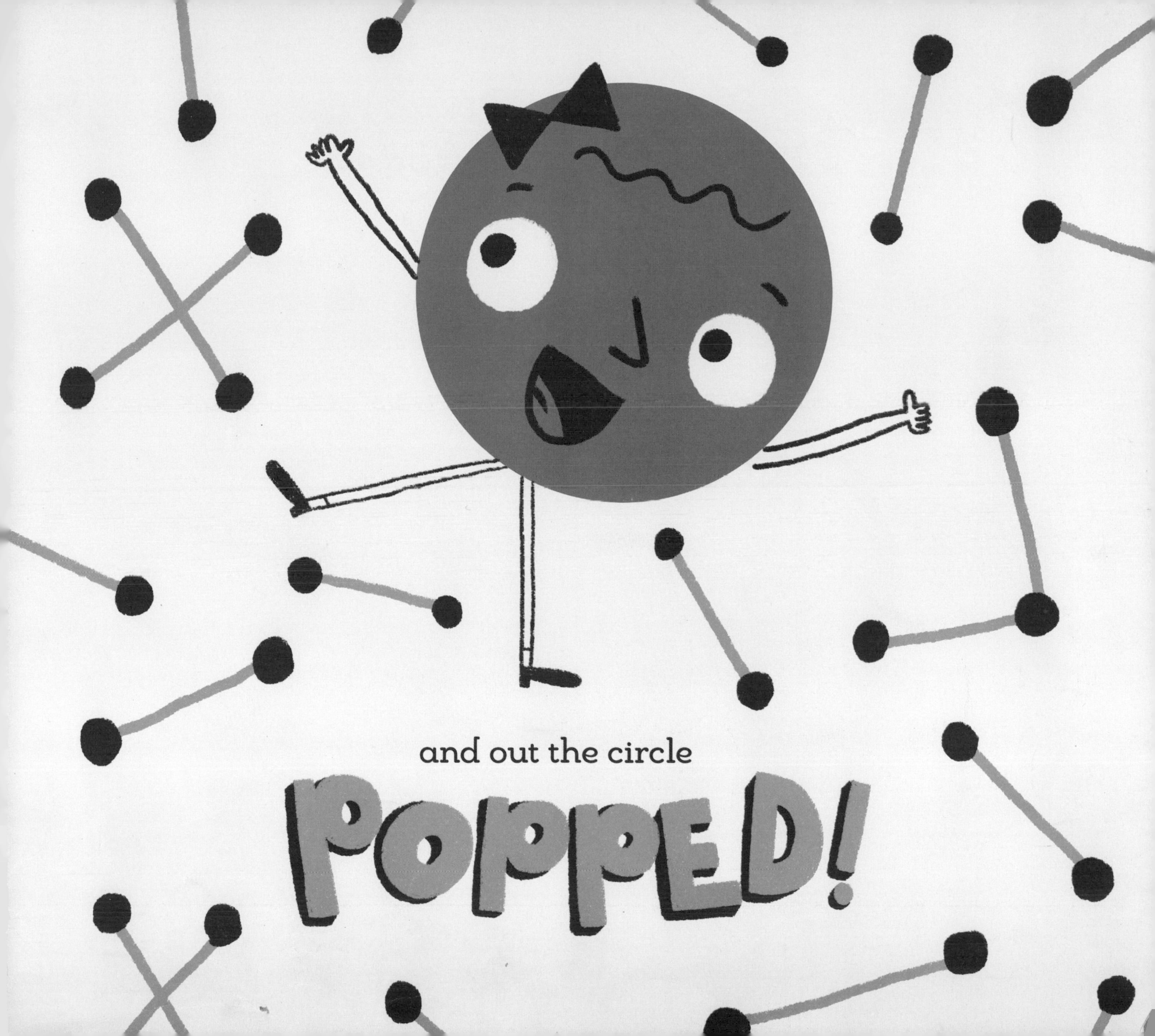
and out the circle
POPPED!

Their lever worked a miracle, and all the shapes were saved.

EVERYBODY held their breath!
The sphere rolled up and hopped.
The prism and the line held tight,

And polygons who heard the scheme

applauded it with glee.

"What a clever LITTLE line!"

a tetrahedron raved.

The line convinced the jungle gym to

make her spaces wider,

so little shapes would not get trapped,
or tangled up inside her.

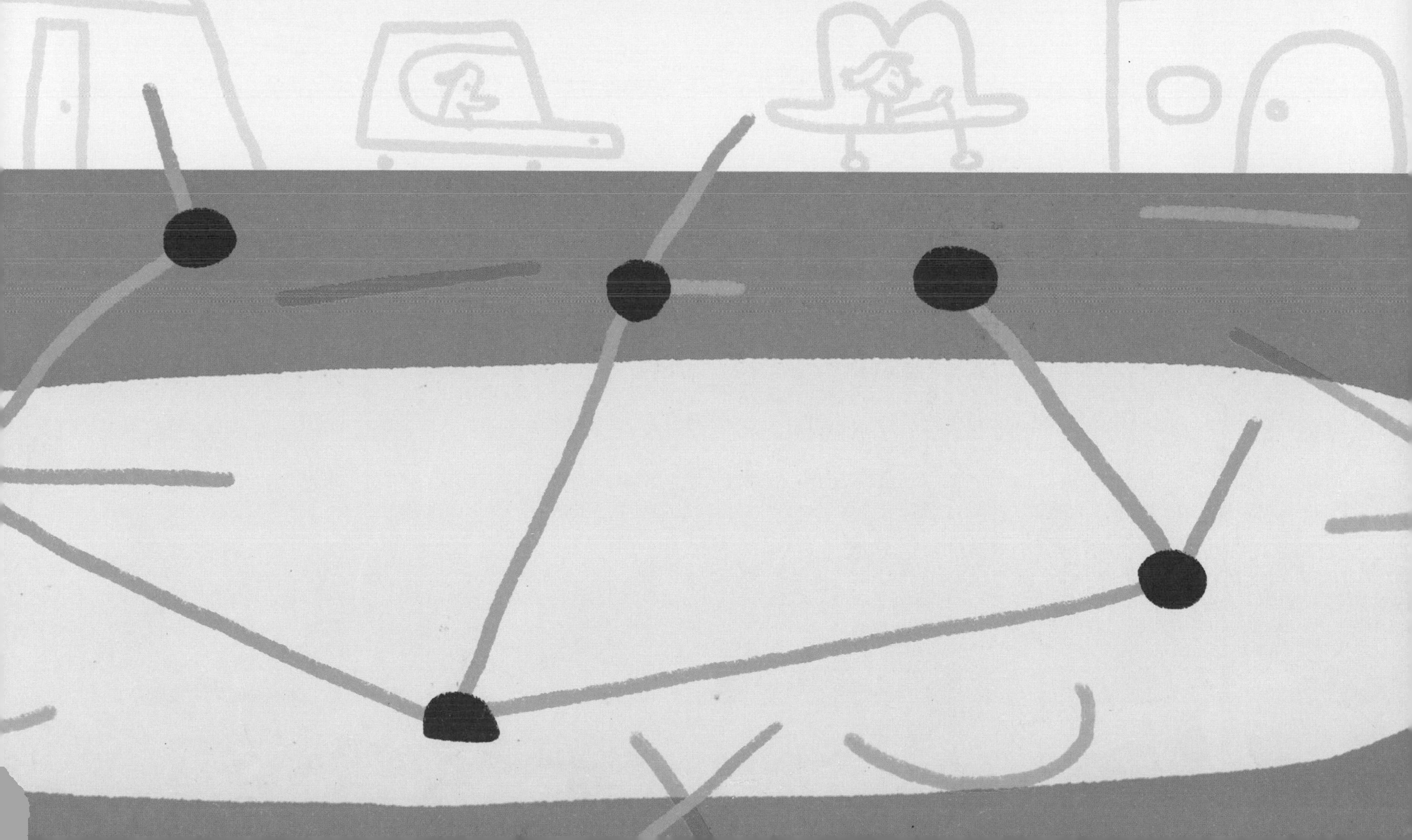

The circle's playing
happily with her
untangled friends.

This geometric tale's
unwound, and now
the story ends.

Gallery of SHAPES

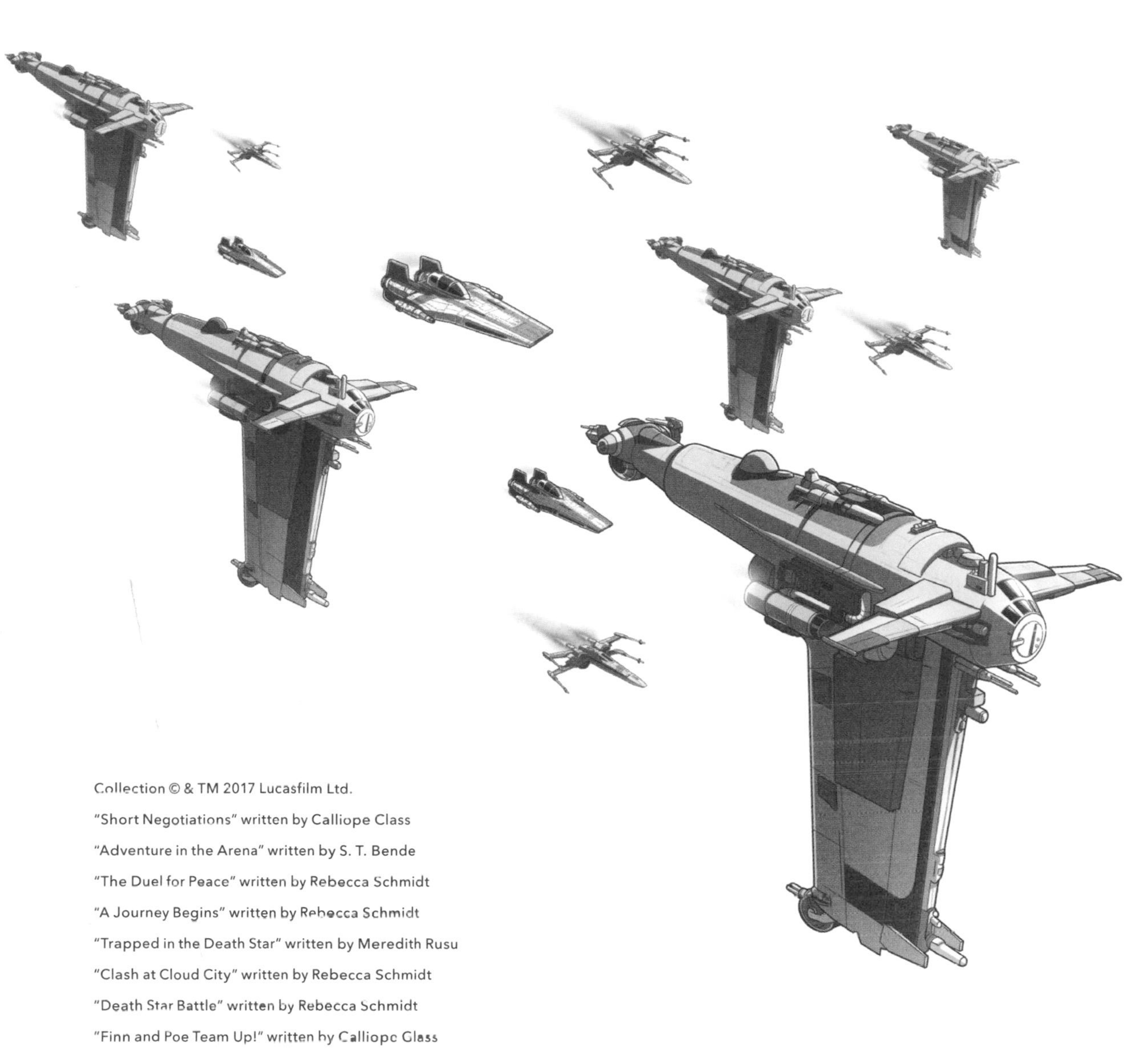

"Short Negotiations" written by Calliope Class
"Adventure in the Arena" written by S. T. Bende
"The Duel for Peace" written by Rebecca Schmidt
"A Journey Begins" written by Rebecca Schmidt
"Trapped in the Death Star" written by Meredith Rusu
"Clash at Cloud City" written by Rebecca Schmidt
"Death Star Battle" written by Rebecca Schmidt
"Finn and Poe Team Up!" written by Calliope Glass
"Mission to Maz" written by S. T. Bende
"The Fight in the Forest" written by Meredith Rusu
"Poe's Plan" written by Ella Patrick
"Captured in Canto Bight" written by Ella Patrick
All illustrations by Pilot Studio

Printed in the United States of America
First Edition, December 2017
10 9 8 7 6 5 4 3
FAC-038091-18243
Library of Congress control number on file.
ISBN 978-1-368-00351-3

Visit the official *Star Wars* website at: www.starwars.com.

STAR WARS
5-MINUTE STORIES STRIKE BACK
Disney
LUCASFILM
PRESS
LOS ANGELES • NEW YORK

STAR
WARS

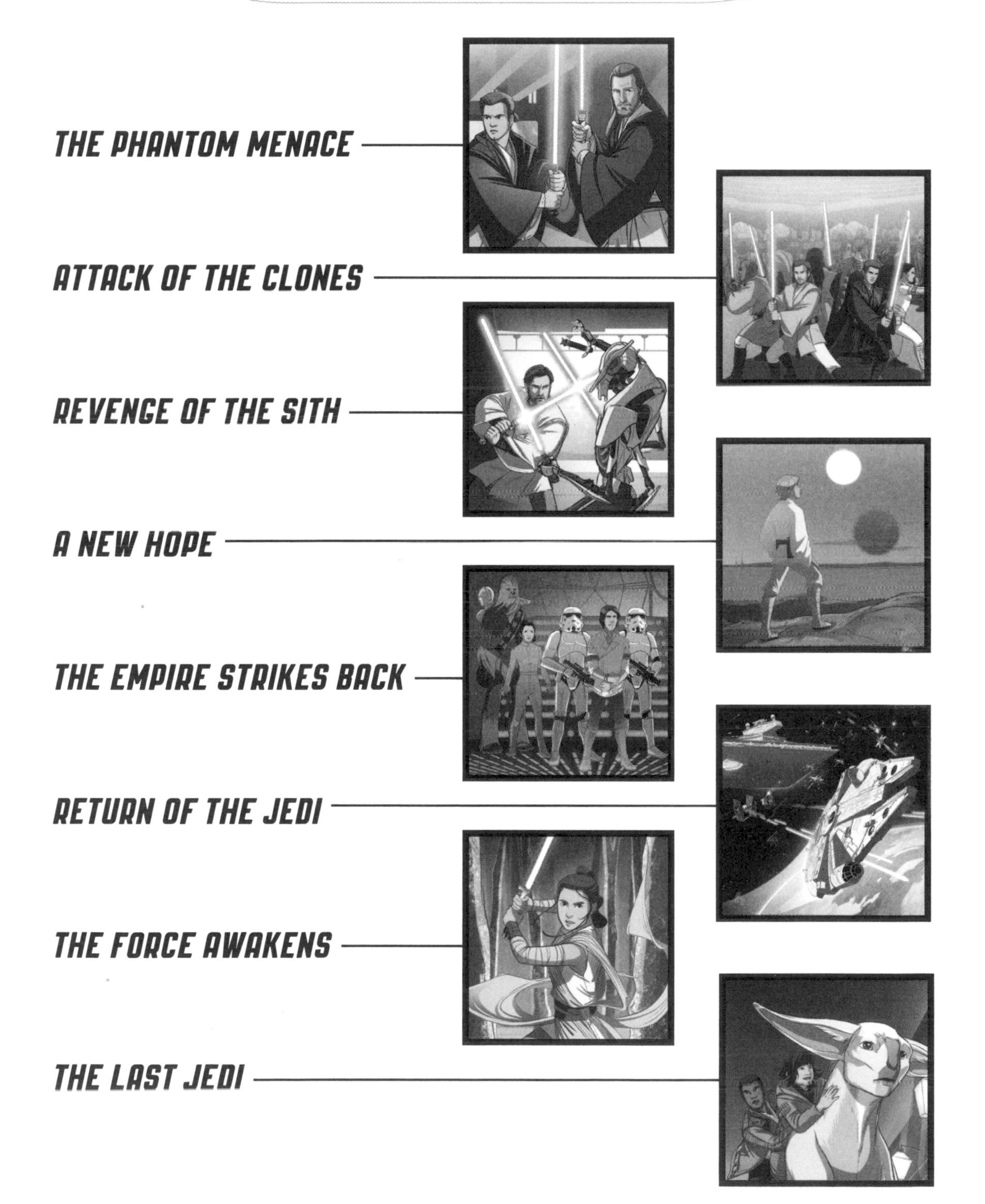
THE PHANTOM MENACE
ATTACK OF THE CLONES
REVENGE OF THE SITH
A NEW HOPE
THE EMPIRE STRIKES BACK
RETURN OF THE JEDI
THE FORCE AWAKENS
THE LAST JEDI

THE PHANTOM MENACE
ATTACK OF THE CLONES
REVENGE OF THE SITH

A NEW HOPE
THE EMPIRE STRIKES BACK
RETURN OF THE JEDI

THE FORCE AWAKENS
THE LAST JEDI

CONTENTS

A long time ago in a galaxy far, far away. . . .

SHORT NEGOTIATIONS

A sleek ship sped through the darkest reaches of space toward the beautiful green planet of Naboo. Inside were two Jedi—a master named Qui-Gon Jinn and an apprentice named Obi-Wan Kenobi. They were on an important mission.

There was trouble in that corner of the galaxy. Although the people of Naboo and their leader, Queen Amidala, were peaceful and kind, the greedy Trade Federation had surrounded the planet with huge battleships. The Trade Federation was using those ships to stop any food or supplies from reaching Naboo. The small planet needed the Jedi's help.

Jedi Master Qui-Gon was confident that the negotiations would be short. He was sure they could convince the Trade Federation to remove its blockade and free Naboo.

What the Jedi didn't know was that the evil Sith Lord Darth Sidious was commanding the Trade Federation . . . and it was about to invade Naboo!

Nobody had expected the Jedi to arrive. The Trade Federation viceroy, who was in charge of the blockade, contacted Darth Sidious to ask what they should do.

"This turn of events is unfortunate," the hologram of Darth Sidious told the viceroy. "We must accelerate our plans. Begin landing your troops."

"And the Jedi?" the viceroy asked.

Darth Sidious ordered the viceroy to get rid of Qui-Gon and Obi-Wan.

The viceroy had poisonous gas pumped into the room where the Jedi were waiting. Qui-Gon and Obi-Wan ignited their lightsabers, but the weapons were no use against the heavy gas that filled the air.

The viceroy sent his battle droids to dispose of the Jedi, but when the droids opened the door, Qui-Gon and Obi-Wan leapt out, ready to fight! They had held their breaths to survive the poisonous gas.

The battle droids were armed with powerful blasters, but the Jedi blocked every shot with their lightsabers. The powerful laser swords flashed and sparks flew as they defeated the droid soldiers.

In a panic the viceroy sealed off the bridge, trying to prevent the Jedi from getting in.

"I want droidekas up here at once!" he cried.

Then the blast doors protecting the bridge slammed shut, too.

But Qui-Gon pressed his lightsaber into the metal and began to cut through.

"Impossible!" cried the viceroy. "This is impossible!"

He hadn't counted on the power of a Jedi's laser sword . . . or the strength of a Jedi's will.

But just as Qui-Gon was about to break through the door to the bridge, two whirling wheels of metal spun into the hallway.

"Master!" Obi-Wan exclaimed. "Destroyer droids!"

The droidekas had arrived and the droids uncoiled from their wheel-like forms. Powerful energy shields appeared around them as they began firing their blasters at the Jedi.

Qui-Gon and Obi-Wan used their lightsabers to block the heavy blasts. The bursts of dangerous light bounced off the Jedi's weapons and raced back toward the deadly destroyers, but the blasts simply fizzled against the droids' shields.

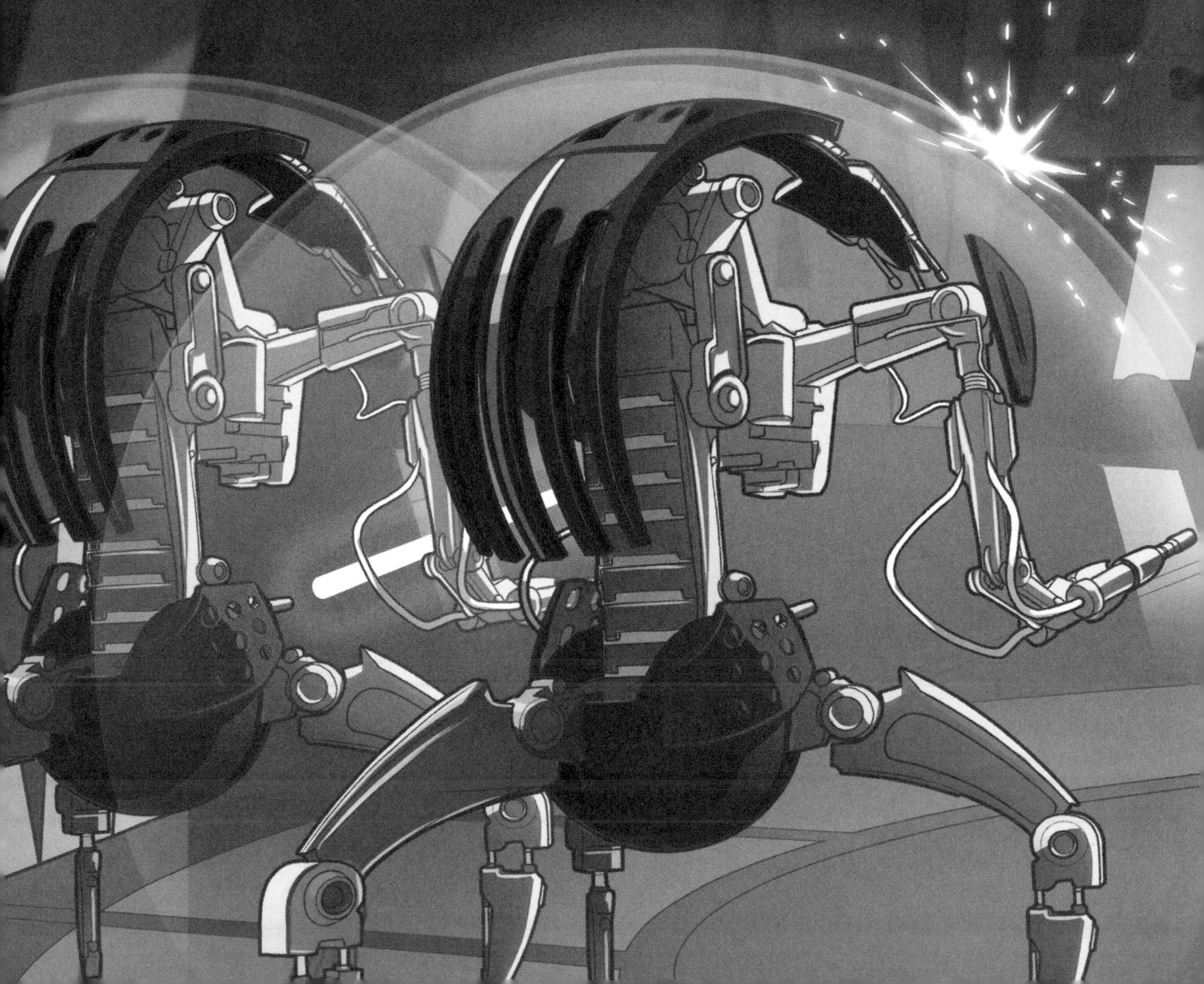

The shield generators were powerful. The destroyer droids were an even match for the Jedi! It was a standoff.

The Jedi decided to outrun the droids. Luckily, their Jedi powers gave them incredible speed.

"Let's go," Qui-Gon told Obi-Wan, and in a sudden blur, the two Jedi fled. By the time the destroyer droids turned to look for them, they were already disappearing around a corner at the other end of a long hallway.

Meanwhile, the Trade Federation's vast army of battle droids, tanks, and warships was preparing to invade Naboo.

Qui-Gon and Obi-Wan traveled through the air vents down to the huge hangar, where they could see the battle droids preparing to leave.

"It's an invasion army!" Obi-Wan exclaimed. Now the Jedi knew the truth: all along the Trade Federation had been gearing up for war.

"We've got to warn the Naboo," Qui-Gon said. "Let's split up. Stow aboard separate ships and meet down on the planet."

Obi-Wan nodded. They had to help. The people of Naboo were peaceful. They had done nothing to deserve this. It would be hard—and dangerous—but that was the life of a Jedi.

Just as the two Jedi were about to part ways, something occurred to Obi-Wan and he smiled.

"You were right about one thing," he told his master. "The negotiations were short."

ADVENTURE IN THE ARENA

Jedi Knight Anakin Skywalker had been in a lot of tricky situations. He'd raced his podracer to freedom and flown a starfighter into battle to save his friends. But when he and Senator Padmé Amidala were captured on an Outer Rim planet called Geonosis, Anakin found himself in his trickiest situation yet. And he didn't know how to get out of it.

Anakin and Padmé had gone to Geonosis to rescue Anakin's Jedi Master, Obi-Wan Kenobi, but they were captured by the bounty hunter Jango Fett and the evil Count Dooku.

Count Dooku was helping his fellow Sith Lord Darth Sidious. They wanted the galaxy to erupt into violence and chaos so they could step in and take control.

Dooku sentenced Anakin, Padmé, and Obi-Wan to fight deadly monsters in a giant arena. The three friends were handcuffed and chained to tall pillars while the Count, Jango Fett, and thousands of Geonosians watched from high above.

Anakin, Padmé, and Obi-Wan exchanged worried looks as three massive creatures stalked into the arena. The first, a red-and-gray horned reek, roared as it lumbered toward Anakin.

"I've got a bad feeling about this," Anakin muttered.

"Concentrate," Obi-Wan suggested as a green insect-like acklay scuttled his way.

Anakin tried to focus, but it was hard as he noticed the sharp quills of the ferocious nexu that was moving toward Padmé.

But the young senator was perfectly capable of taking care of herself. Padmé first used a pin to undo her handcuffs. Then she used her strength to climb to the top of the pillar and beat back the nexu with the heavy chain that had been attached to her wrists.

Anakin outsmarted the reek. When the beast charged, Anakin jumped onto its back. The reek reared back, breaking the chain from the pillar and freeing Anakin. Now he could help his friends!

Anakin steered the reek toward Padmé's pillar so she could jump down onto the reek's back.

Obi-Wan used his speed to avoid the acklay. He zigzagged as the creature's sharp pincers pierced everything in sight, including the chain that bound Obi-Wan to his pillar.

When the acklay knocked over the heavy stone column, Obi-Wan quickly rolled out of the way and ran as fast as he could.

Anakin and Padmé steered the reek over to Obi-Wan, and the Jedi Master jumped onto the reek's back, holding on tight to Padmé and Anakin.

Anakin tried to steer the creature to safety . . . but a group of deadly droidekas rolled into the arena.

The three friends were trapped again!

A flash of purple sparked from the balcony as Jedi Master Mace Windu's lightsaber zapped to life.

"This party's over," the Jedi Master said, pointing the fiery blade at Count Dooku and Jango Fett.

The hum of lightsabers filled the arena. Dozens of blue and green blades blazed with power! Anakin looked around in relief. Mace Windu and the Jedi Knights had come to save the day!

"You're impossibly outnumbered," Count Dooku said calmly.

The Sith Lord was right. On the arena floor, hundreds of battle droids marched toward Anakin, Padmé, and Obi-Wan. But Mace Windu knew the power of the Force. He and his fellow Jedi leapt down to join the three friends, and together they pushed back the army of droids.

The arena was filled with streaks of blue and green light as the Jedi deflected blasts with their lightsabers.

The Force was strong with them!

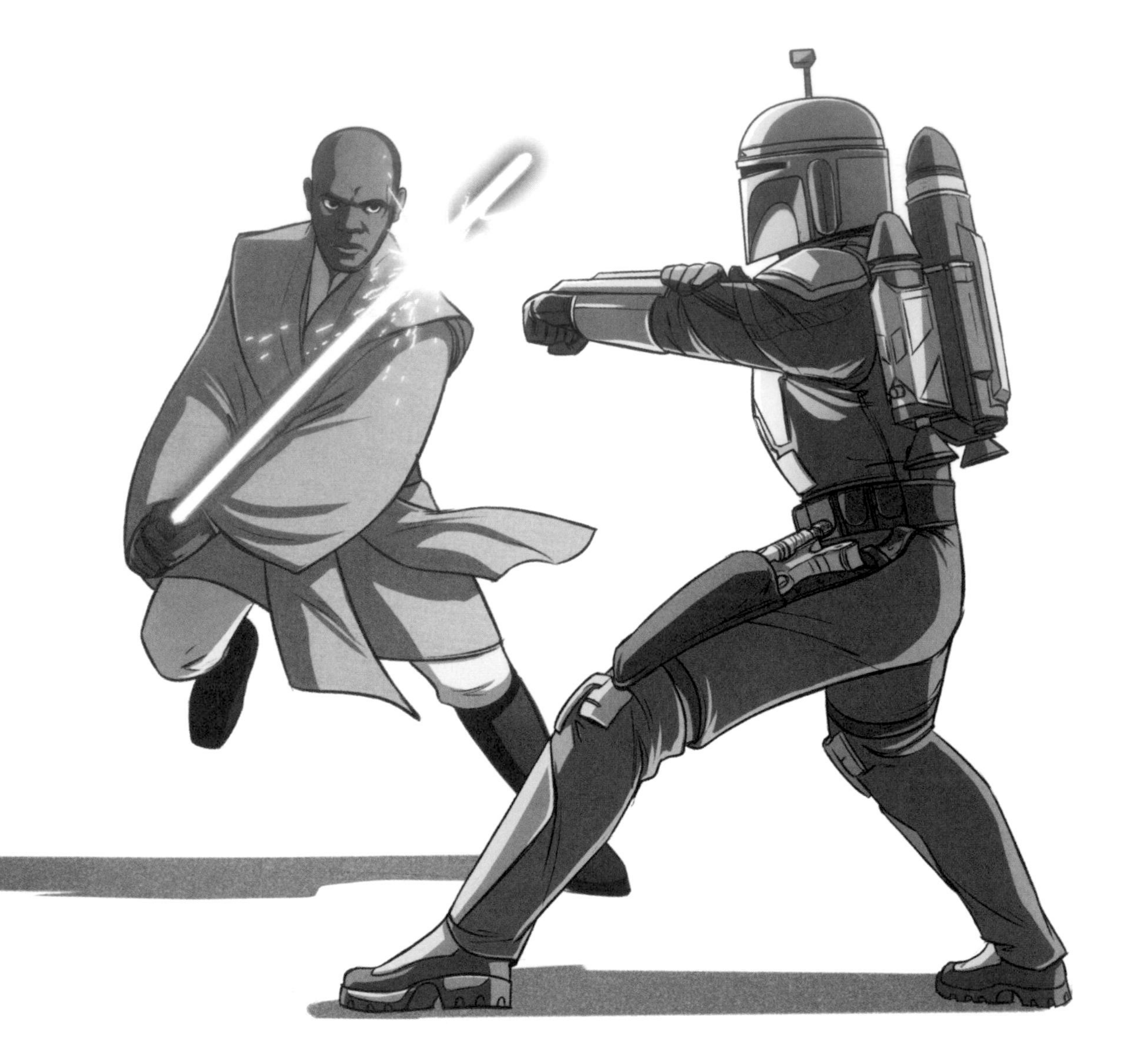

When Jango Fett saw what was happening, he fired up his jetpack and flew to the arena floor.

But Mace Windu was ready for the bounty hunter. He charged, angling his lightsaber to deflect Jango's blasts, and stopped Jango's attack once and for all with one powerful swing.

But the battle droids soon closed in, and Anakin, Padmé, Obi-Wan, Mace, and the rest of the Jedi drew together in a defensive circle. They raised their weapons, but Count Dooku called off the battle!

"You have fought gallantly," Count Dooku praised. "Now, surrender and your lives will be spared."

The Jedi refused to surrender. Count Dooku gave the signal, and the droids raised their blasters. As the Jedi prepared for one final attack, Padmé pointed to the sky and cried out.

"Look!"

Ships swooped in from the clouds.

Master Yoda had brought a clone army to rescue the Jedi!

Anakin, Padmé, Obi-Wan, and the rest of the Jedi quickly boarded the transports and flew to safety.

Escaping the arena had been one of the trickiest things Anakin had ever done! He knew he still needed to find a way to stop Count Dooku, but he also knew something very important: no matter what the future had in store, Anakin and his friends would face it together!

THE DUEL FOR PEACE

Jedi Master Obi-Wan Kenobi peered down from the shadows. It had been a long time since he'd last seen Count Dooku's second-in-command, General Grievous, but he would recognize the cyborg's mechanical cough anywhere.

Obi-Wan was on the small planet of Utapau. The Jedi Council had sent him to stop Grievous and his Separatist comrades, whose evil plans had caused the galaxy to erupt into war and chaos.

Obi-Wan's apprentice, Anakin Skywalker, had finally defeated Count Dooku, but Grievous still stood in the way of peace. It was Obi-Wan's job to put an end to the evil cyborg once and for all.

Obi-Wan used the element of surprise to his advantage.

Leaping down from above, the Jedi landed right in front of the general and a number of his droid soldiers.

"Hello there," Obi-Wan said with a smile.

Attack droids ran toward the Jedi Master, electrostaffs blazing. But Obi-Wan used the Force, and with a mighty crash a huge piece of machinery fell from the ceiling—right onto the droids!

"Back away," General Grievous ordered his troops. "I will deal with this Jedi slime myself."

"Your move," Obi-Wan said.

General Grievous shrugged off his cloak, extended his four menacing arms, and ignited a lightsaber in each mechanical hand. The evil cyborg had taken the powerful weapons from the Jedi he had defeated in the past.

Obi-Wan would not allow Grievous to do the same with *his* lightsaber.

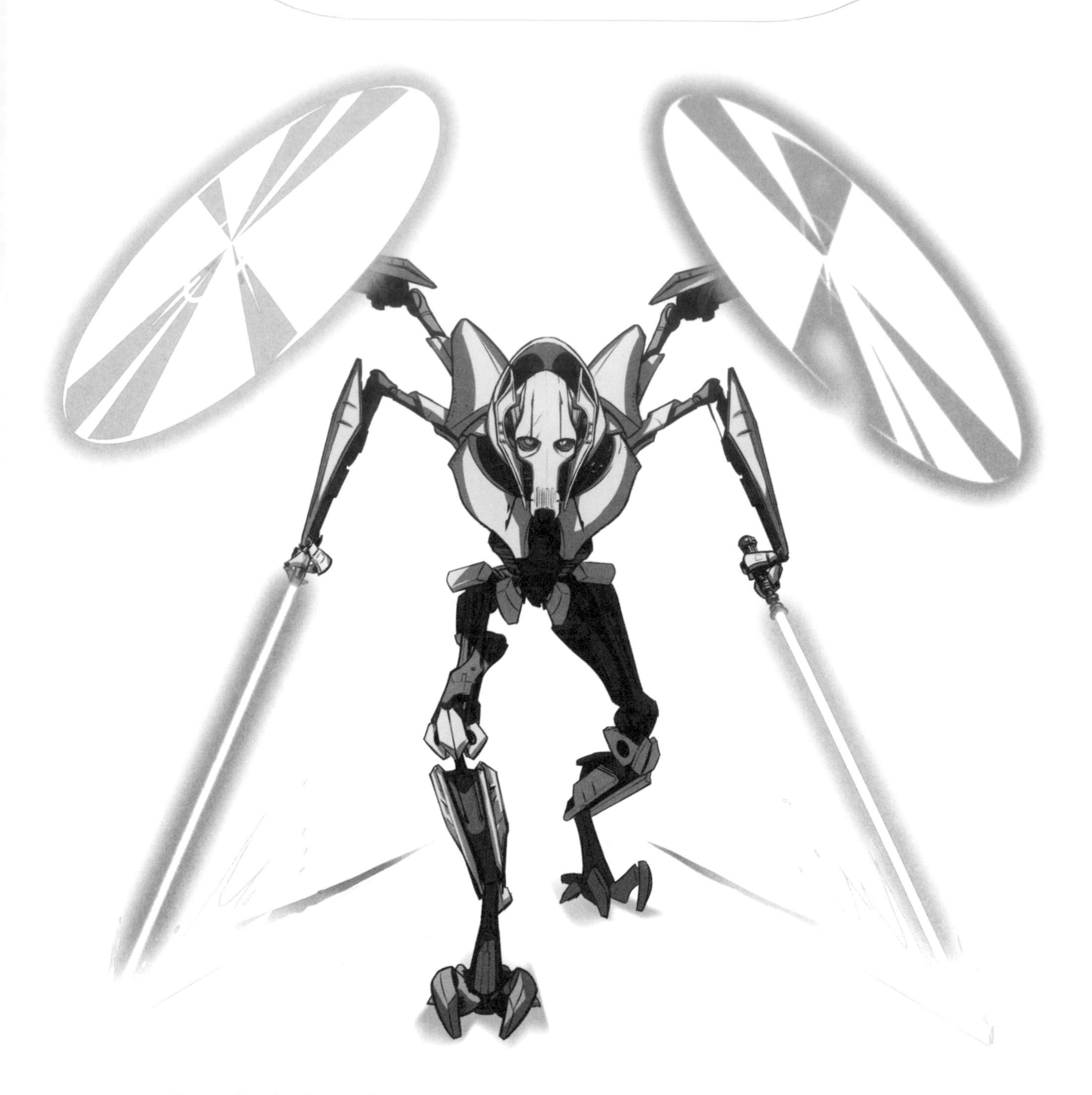

"You fool. I have been trained in your Jedi arts by Count Dooku," the cyborg scoffed.

General Grievous spun his lightsabers, burning the floor beneath him. He strode closer and closer to Obi-Wan, his weapons a blur of light.

Grievous may have been trained by Count Dooku, but Obi-Wan had studied under Master Yoda and Qui-Gon Jinn. Their teachings had taught him patience and how to trust the Force, but they had also trained him how to use a lightsaber. The Jedi Master raised his blade, slashing it against two of the general's.

The cyborg battled back, but Obi-Wan's lightsaber was always there. It wasn't long before Obi-Wan had destroyed all but two of Grievous's lightsabers.

Suddenly, the Republic's clone army arrived to help! They were there to take down Grievous's droid soldiers.

"Army or not, you must realize you are doomed," the general told Obi-Wan.

"Oh, I don't think so," said Obi-Wan.

With a mighty Force push, Obi-Wan threw General Grievous back. The cyborg hit the ground hard but not hard enough. He saw his chance to flee.

Grievous raced to his large wheel bike and steered it away from the battle.

Obi-Wan couldn't let General Grievous escape. He whistled for his own ride, a lizard named Boga. The Jedi Master chased after the general, but Grievous had zoomed ahead.

Then, Boga lost her footing and Obi-Wan's lightsaber flew out of his hand!

If Obi-Wan stopped to retrieve it, he'd lose his chance to catch General Grievous. But the thought of facing the cyborg without his lightsaber was certainly unsettling.

However, Obi-Wan knew he could trust the Force. Leaving his lightsaber behind, the Jedi raced on to catch up with Grievous.

Obi-Wan and General Grievous entered Utapau's inner tunnels. Obi-Wan had just caught up to the general when the Separatist leader raised an electrostaff. Obi-Wan leapt over to the cyborg's vehicle, narrowly avoiding Grievous's strike!

As the wheel bike careened around tight corners and past deep canyons, the two opponents battled for the upper hand.

Suddenly, the wheel bike spun out of control and flew off the side of a large platform, almost taking Obi-Wan and General Grievous with it! But they both leapt off just in time.

Obi-Wan fell hard. He rolled over, holding the electrostaff as Grievous raised a blaster. The Jedi Master blocked the blast and knocked the weapon out of Grievous's hand, but a mighty push from the Separatist leader sent the staff flying from Obi-Wan's grip.

Down to hand-to-hand combat, Grievous knocked Obi-Wan back. The Jedi flew off the platform! He reached out, grabbing the edge just in time. General Grievous laughed. His victory was nearly complete.

But General Grievous had forgotten about the blaster. Obi-Wan reached for it using the Force and blasted the general just in time. Grievous had finally been defeated.

Obi-Wan pulled himself up from the edge and threw the blaster away.

"So uncivilized," the Jedi Master said.

With Grievous gone, the war could finally end. Obi-Wan smiled. Now he just needed to find his lightsaber.

A JOURNEY BEGINS

The droids C-3PO and R2-D2 were having a bad day.

The evil Empire—led by the Sith Lord Darth Sidious and his second-in command, Darth Vader—had taken control of the galaxy.

Imperial stormtroopers had attacked C-3PO and R2-D2's ship, and the droids had only narrowly escaped Vader's clutches. Now they were stranded on the desert planet of Tatooine with no hope of rescue.

"I've got to rest before I fall apart," C-3PO complained.

R2-D2 turned down a dark, rocky path.

"Where do you think you're going? This way is much easier," C-3PO said, pointing in the opposite direction.

But R2-D2 just beeped back at his friend. He was on a mission, and he couldn't be stopped.

"What mission? What are you talking about?" C-3PO asked.

R2 wouldn't answer, so the golden droid refused to follow him. Soon the little blue-and-white astromech droid had left C-3PO far behind.

But the rocky path was dangerous, and R2-D2 rolled right into a trap. With an electrified blast, a small Jawa scavenger froze R2-D2. The droid couldn't move!

Jawas carried R2-D2 to their sandcrawler. The little droid was surrounded by salvaged junk and other strange droids. R2 was worried. Where were the Jawas taking him?

Luckily, R2-D2 wouldn't have to find out alone. The Jawas had captured C-3PO, too!

The two friends stayed close together as the sandcrawler stopped and the Jawas lined up the droids outside. The droids were going to be sold.

An older man, Owen Lars, and his young nephew, Luke Skywalker, examined the droids. The man motioned to C-3PO and a small red droid.

"Luke, take these two over to the garage. I want them cleaned up before dinner," he said.

Luke led C-3PO away. R2-D2 beeped in alarm. He didn't want to be separated from his friend again!

Suddenly, the red droid started to spark. It was broken. C-3PO convinced Luke to choose R2-D2 instead.

"Now, don't you forget this!" C-3PO said to R2-D2 as the droids followed Luke. "Why I should stick my neck out for you is quite beyond my capacity."

As he was cleaning the droids, Luke found something jammed in R2-D2's data card input. He tugged and pulled, and suddenly a small hologram appeared. The hologram showed a young woman who looked very important.

"Help me, Obi-Wan Kenobi. You're my only hope," she said.

Luke asked R2-D2 where he had gotten the message, but R2 wouldn't answer.

Luke asked his aunt and uncle about Obi-Wan Kenobi at dinner.

The only Kenobi Luke knew was Ben Kenobi, an old man who had lived out in the desert near Luke's family for as long as Luke could remember.

But Luke's uncle told him to ignore the message. He needed Luke to help on the farm, not to be thinking about strange messages and planets and people far away.

Luke was frustrated. He walked outside and watched as the suns set beyond the desert. He had hoped that R2-D2's message would be the start of an exciting adventure that would take him away from the boring life he had always known. But it looked like he would be stuck on Tatooine forever.

Luke was destined for adventure after all.

R2-D2 had escaped!

"I told him not to go," C-3PO told Luke. "But he's faulty, kept babbling on about his mission!"

Luke couldn't believe it. If his uncle found out he had lost one of the new droids, Luke would be in big trouble.

Early the next morning, Luke and C-3PO raced into the desert to find R2-D2.

They caught up to the astromech droid, but suddenly, dangerous Sand People attacked them!

Luke was about to be captured when a loud sound echoed across the rocks. Startled, the Sand People looked up to see a strange robed figure quickly approaching. The frightened Sand People ran away!

R2-D2 whistled in alarm as the figure approached Luke. But when the figure lowered its hood, a man's friendly face was revealed.

"Hello there!" the man said. "Don't be afraid."

"Ben? Ben Kenobi?" Luke asked. The old man nodded and revealed that he was also known as Obi-Wan Kenobi!

R2-D2 beeped. His mission was almost complete.

Obi-Wan led Luke and the droids to his small hut. He told Luke he used to be a Jedi Knight and had fought beside Luke's father during the Clone Wars.

The Jedi had all disappeared long before, but they had once fought for peace and justice in the galaxy using a mysterious energy field called the Force.

Luke didn't know much about Jedi Knights—or his father, for that matter, though.

"He was a good friend," Obi-Wan said. "Which reminds me, I have something here for you."

Obi-Wan gave Luke his father's lightsaber. The blade ignited with a *whoosh!* Luke smiled. The lightsaber felt right in his hand, as if he was meant to have it.

Obi-Wan turned to R2-D2. It was time to find out what the young woman's message was.

With a simple push of a button, the hologram reappeared. But this time R2-D2 played the full message.

The young woman, Princess Leia, was part of the Rebellion that was fighting against the evil Empire.

R2-D2 and C-3PO had been on board Leia's ship before it was captured by Darth Vader.

Princess Leia had hidden important information in R2-D2's memory banks before the two droids escaped. She needed Obi-Wan to take R2-D2 safely to her home planet of Alderaan to help the Rebellion.

Obi-Wan asked Luke to go along with him on this new mission and become a Jedi like his father before him.

Luke agreed to help Obi-Wan and R2-D2. He didn't know what was going to happen next, but he knew that his life was about to change forever.

TRAPPED IN THE DEATH STAR

Deep in space, Darth Sidious, Darth Vader, and their evil Empire had built a terrible weapon. It was called the Death Star. This battle station was as big as a moon and could destroy planets with a single laser beam.

The Empire wanted to use the Death Star to secure its control over the galaxy.

Little did the Empire know, the Rebellion had a plan to stop it.

Luke Skywalker, the droids R2-D2 and C-3PO, Han Solo, and Chewbacca the Wookiee were delivering secret information about the Death Star from Princess Leia to the rebels on the planet of Alderaan.

Jedi Master Obi-Wan Kenobi, also known as Ben, was with them. He was training Luke to become a great Jedi.

The heroes flew to Alderaan in Han's ship, the *Millennium Falcon.*

But when they arrived, the planet had been destroyed! The dreaded Death Star loomed in its place.

The terrible space station locked on to the *Millennium Falcon* with a tractor beam.

"It's pulling us in!" cried Han.

Thinking fast, the heroes hid in secret cargo compartments on board Han and Chewie's ship. Stormtroopers from the Death Star boarded the *Falcon*, but they didn't find the friends. They were safe—for now.

Han said they needed to shut down the tractor beam to escape.

Just then, he got a clever idea. If they disguised themselves as stormtroopers, they could sneak aboard the Death Star and find the tractor beam's power source and turn it off.

Han tricked two more stormtroopers to come onto the *Millennium Falcon*, and he and Luke knocked them out. They put on the armor, and the group hurried to the space station's computer.

R2-D2 located the tractor beam's power source. Ben said he would go shut it down.

Luke wanted to go with him, but Ben told him he must stay.

"The Force will be with you, always," Ben said.

As soon as Ben left, R2-D2 discovered something else on the Death Star's computer. Princess Leia was a prisoner aboard the space station!

"We have to save her!" exclaimed Luke.

He, Han, and Chewie raced to the detention level. Han stood guard while Luke found Leia's cell and opened the door.

"I'm Luke Skywalker," he said. "I'm here to rescue you!"

Luke, Han, Leia, and Chewie zipped down the hall. But they wouldn't be able to escape so easily. Their path back to Han's ship was blocked by dozens of stormtroopers.

Thinking fast, Princess Leia used a blaster to shoot a hole in a wall grate. Now *she* was rescuing *them*!

"Into the garbage chute!" Leia yelled.

The friends slid into a giant smelly pile of garbage.

Han was *not* happy. But at least they had gotten away. Then . . .

Rummmble!

The trash compactor walls began closing in. The friends would be crushed!

Luke called C-3PO over his comlink.

"Shut down all the garbage mashers on the detention level!"

R2-D2 stopped the compactor just in time! The friends cheered.

But they were still trapped in the Death Star. They needed to get back to Han's ship and escape before the stormtroopers found them again.

By the time they climbed out of the garbage masher, *all* the stormtroopers had been alerted to their presence. Now the heroes' path was blocked by more enemies than ever!

Bravely, Han and Chewie ran straight at the stormtroopers.

"Get back to the ship!" Han cried to Luke and Leia before chasing the enemies.

The stormtroopers retreated!

Meanwhile, Luke and Leia raced in the opposite direction. But stormtroopers trapped them on a ledge over a deep chasm. They were stuck again!

This time, Luke had an idea. . . .

He used a cable on his belt to swing them to safety!

The stormtroopers didn't have cables, so they couldn't follow Luke and Leia.

The friends were almost free!

Not far away, Ben had reached the machine powering the tractor beam and shut it down. The *Millennium Falcon* could fly away from the Death Star.

Ben needed to get back to the others, but Darth Vader blocked his path!

"I've been waiting for you, Obi-Wan," said Vader.

It had been many years since anyone had called Ben by that name. Long before, back when Darth Vader had been known as Anakin Skywalker, Ben had trained him as a Jedi Knight. But then Anakin had turned to the dark side.

"We meet again, at last," Vader said.

Vader lit up his red lightsaber. Ben lit up his blue one.

"When I left you, I was but the learner," said Vader. "Now I am the master."

"Only a master of evil, Darth," said Ben.

They began to battle. Their lightsabers fizzled and crackled as they fought.

"Your powers are weak, old man," Darth Vader taunted.

"You can't win, Darth," Ben warned. "If you strike me down I shall become more powerful than you can possibly imagine."

But Darth Vader didn't listen. He struck Ben with his lightsaber, and the old Jedi Master disappeared.

Ben became one with the Force.

All the stormtroopers guarding Han's ship had turned to watch the fight. While they were distracted, the heroes started sneaking aboard the *Millennium Falcon*.

But Luke saw what happened to Ben.

"No!" he cried.

He started to run toward Darth Vader. He would fight the Dark Lord himself!

"Luke, it's too late!" Leia shouted at him.

They needed to escape while they could.

Luke knew Leia was right. He joined his friends, and in a whirl of engines and light, the *Millennium Falcon* zoomed away.

The heroes had escaped!

But Luke was very sad. He had wanted Ben to escape, too. He thought he needed Ben to continue his Jedi training.

Luke, Leia, Han, Chewie, and the droids still needed to complete their mission and deliver the secret plans to the Rebellion. It was the only way to save the galaxy. Luke was more determined than ever to help the Rebellion succeed.

He would do it for Ben.

CLASH AT CLOUD CITY

Leia stepped off the *Millennium Falcon* and quickly studied her surroundings. She and her friends Han, Chewbacca, and the droid C-3PO had landed on the floating Cloud City after barely escaping Darth Vader and the Empire.

Han's old friend Lando Calrissian ran all of Cloud City. Han promised his team that they would be safe there. But Leia couldn't help worrying.

"How you doing, you old pirate? So good to see you!" Lando said to Han.

Leia tried to enjoy the beautiful city in the clouds, but she sensed that something was wrong. The next morning, Lando led the group to breakfast.

Darth Vader was waiting for them with the fearsome bounty hunter Boba Fett—son of the famous warrior Jango Fett!

It had all been a trap.

Han fired his blaster, but the Sith Lord easily swatted away the bolts as stormtroopers swarmed Leia and her friends.

"I'm sorry," Lando called to Han.

The Empire had made him betray his friend.

But Han just clenched Leia's hand tight.

There was no escape this time.

Leia and her friends were taken deep into Cloud City. Lando revealed that they were all bait for Luke, who was far away training to become a Jedi.

Darth Vader knew that Luke would come to help his friends, and when he did, Vader planned to freeze the young Jedi in carbonite and deliver him to the Emperor, Lord Sidious.

But Darth Vader wanted to test the carbonite system on Han first.

Leia had never felt so powerless as she watched Han being led away.

"I love you!" Leia said.

"I know," Han replied.

With a huge screech and a blast of carbonite, Han was frozen.

"He's alive," Lando said, checking Han's vitals. "And in perfect hibernation." The carbonite system had worked.

Leia and her companions were pulled away to be taken back to Darth Vader's ship. Han Solo was given to Boba Fett to be delivered to the vile gangster Jabba the Hutt.

As Leia looked back at Han's frozen face, she wondered if she would ever see him again.

Darth Vader had been right about Luke. As soon as he had sensed his friends were in danger, he traveled to Cloud City. Leia saw Luke right before the Imperial stormtroopers pulled her away.

"Luke! Luke, don't!" Leia called. "It's a trap! It's a trap!"

Luke knew his friends would never be safe until Darth Vader was defeated. The young Jedi searched Cloud City until he found the Sith Lord.

"The Force is strong with you, young Skywalker," Darth Vader said, raising his red lightsaber. "But you are not a Jedi yet."

Luke ignited his blue lightsaber. Their blades clashed. Darth Vader pushed Luke into the carbonite chamber, but Luke leapt free just in time.

"Impressive," Darth Vader said. "Most impressive."

Meanwhile, Leia, Chewie, and C-3PO were still in danger. They had almost reached the Imperial ship when suddenly their captors were attacked. Lando was rescuing them!

The team battled their way back to the *Millennium Falcon* and zoomed away from Cloud City.

Darth Vader forced Luke back and back until there was nowhere for Luke to go. "There is no escape," Darth Vader said.

Luke looked down into the huge chasm beneath him. There had to be a way out of this.

"Join me and I will complete your training," Darth Vader told Luke.

"I'll never join you!" Luke said.

Darth Vader reached out to Luke.

"I am your father," he said.

Luke couldn't believe it. The Jedi Master Obi-Wan Kenobi had told Luke that his father was a Jedi hero, *destroyed* by Darth Vader.

"Join me, and together we can rule the galaxy as father and son," Darth Vader said.

Luke had so many questions. But he knew one thing for sure: Darth Vader had hurt his friends over and over again. He could never join the villain. Luke let go and fell into the huge chasm beneath him. He fell until he grabbed on to an antenna at the very bottom of Cloud City.

"Leia! Leia!" Luke called out.

Far away on the *Falcon*, Leia couldn't stop feeling that Luke needed her. She knew that turning back would put them in danger once again, but she couldn't abandon her friend.

"We've got to go back," she told Lando and Chewie.

They piloted the ship back to Cloud City.

"Look, someone's up there!" Lando said, pointing to a small figure hanging from an antenna.

It was Luke!

Lando raced to the airlock and rescued Luke just in time. Leia hugged her friend close as Lando and Chewie piloted the *Falcon* to safety.

Back with the Rebellion, Leia and Luke thought about all the work ahead of them. They had to rescue Han from Jabba the Hutt, and they had to find a way to stop Darth Vader once and for all.

Together, however, they might just have a chance.

DEATH STAR BATTLE

Not a scratch, Lando thought as he powered up the *Millennium Falcon* and flew into position.

The Rebellion had a chance to surprise the Empire and destroy the new Death Star before it was finished, just like it had destroyed the first Death Star years before.

Lando knew it would be a tough battle, but he had promised his friend Han Solo that he would take care of Han's ship, the *Millennium Falcon*, and Lando wasn't going to let his friend down again.

Lando heard Admiral Ackbar's voice through his comlink: "All crafts, prepare to jump into hyperspace on my mark."

Lando punched in the coordinates to Endor, the small forest moon near the new Death Star. He had a good copilot, an alien named Nien Nunb, but Lando still wished his friend Han was with him.

But Han Solo was on a secret mission to bring down the Death Star's shields from the forests of Endor. If he didn't succeed, Lando and the rest of the Rebellion wouldn't be able to destroy the new Death Star.

Admiral Ackbar commanded the fleet to advance, and as one, all the ships leapt into hyperspace.

In what seemed like moments, Lando found himself right in front of the skeleton of the new Death Star. He stared in awe. It was bigger than he could ever have imagined.

"All wings report in," Lando ordered the fleet.

"Red Leader standing by," said Wedge Antilles, adjusting his controls a little. Unlike Lando, Wedge had seen a Death Star before. And this time, Wedge planned to fire the shot that destroyed it.

Lando prepared for their surprise attack on the new Death Star, but Nien shouted in alarm. The sensors were jammed!

"How could they be jamming us if they don't know . . . if we're coming?" Lando said.

Suddenly, he realized the Rebellion had made a mistake. The Emperor, Darth Sidious, had known they were coming all along.

"Break off the attack!" he ordered.

Wedge checked his own sensors, but there was nothing there.

"I get no reading. You sure?" he asked Lando.

Just then, an entire fleet of the Emperor's forces appeared out of nowhere. The rebel fleet was completely outnumbered.

"Take evasive action," cried Admiral Ackbar from his command ship. "It's a trap!"

Imperial TIE fighters raced toward the rebel fleet, firing blast after blast. Wedge and his fellow rebel X-wing pilots zoomed past Lando to fight back.

Not a scratch, Lando thought as he maneuvered the *Falcon* into attack position. Just then, a huge blast came from the Death Star, destroying a rebel ship. The *Falcon* rocked from the blast, and Lando looked up at the Death Star in amazement. It was still under construction. It wasn't supposed to be operational yet!

"All craft prepare to retreat," Admiral Ackbar ordered. The rebels didn't stand a chance now that the Death Star's powerful laser was working.

Lando knew they wouldn't have another opportunity to destroy this new Death Star. Besides, Han would deactivate the shields down on Endor. He just needed more time. Han wouldn't let them down!

Lando ordered the rebel fleet to move closer to the Imperial forces. They wouldn't last long against the Star Destroyers, but Lando knew they wouldn't survive another second against the Death Star with its shields still up. And the Death Star wouldn't fire at its own ships.

Wedge flew through the Imperial fleet, trying to take down as many TIE fighters as he could. But there was always another ship to fight. The Empire's forces seemed endless.

Just then, the shields of the Death Star came down. Han's mission was a success!

"Ha-ha-ha, I told you he'd do it!" Lando told Nien Nunb.

It was finally time to attack the Death Star.

"Here goes nothing!" Lando cried.

The *Millennium Falcon* flew through a gap in the Imperial defenses and into the Death Star. Wedge followed close behind. But the rebels weren't alone. TIE fighters raced after them, firing blast after blast!

Wedge and Lando battled their way to the heart of the Death Star. There, right in front of them, was the power generator.

Wedge took a deep breath and fired a round at the Death Star's weak point. Lando fired after him and then smiled in awe as the reactor exploded.

They had done it!

But Lando and Wedge were still in trouble. They raced back toward open space, but the Death Star was collapsing around them. Just before the entrance closed, Wedge and the *Millennium Falcon* escaped.

"Yee-haw!" Lando cried.

Behind them, the Emperor's ultimate weapon exploded. The rebel fleet had won!

Lando and all his Rebellion friends celebrated their victory on the moon of Endor. Lando looked everywhere until he saw his friend Han.

Not a scratch, he thought as he gave his friend a hug. *Not a scratch*.

FINN AND POE TEAM UP!

Poe Dameron was the best pilot in the Resistance. He flew an X-wing starship, and with his faithful droid, BB-8, at his back, nobody could catch him!

The Resistance was fighting the First Order—a sinister organization that had risen out of the ashes of the evil Empire. The Rebellion had defeated the Empire many years earlier. But now the First Order was on the rise, and the Resistance was getting desperate.

General Leia Organa led the Resistance. She was a brilliant, respected leader, but she was worried that she wouldn't be able to defeat the First Order without her brother, the Jedi Master Luke Skywalker. Nobody knew where Luke was, as he had disappeared many years before.

General Organa personally chose Poe Dameron to help her track down Luke. Poe's mission was to go to a man named Lor San Tekka on the desert planet of Jakku. Leia hoped that Lor might have information that could help lead them to Luke Skywalker.

Soon Poe and BB-8 had found Lor San Tekka.

"This will begin to make things right," the old man told Poe, handing him a data chip that contained a map to Luke. "Without the Jedi, there can be no balance in the Force."

But just then, BB-8 rolled into Lor's hut, beeping frantically.

"We've got company," Poe said grimly. The First Order had arrived.

Outside the little desert village, a large transport had landed and First Order troopers were spilling out of it. They were also searching for the map to Luke Skywalker. General Organa wasn't the only person looking for Luke. Kylo Ren—a warrior with the First Order who was strong in the dark side of the Force—wanted to find the Jedi Knight and destroy him.

Poe saw the First Order stormtroopers attacking the town and knew that he needed to help the innocent villagers. But he couldn't risk the map falling into the hands of the First Order. The fate of the galaxy depended on it!

So Poe gave the data chip to BB-8.

"It's safer with you than it is with me," Poe told his droid. "You get as far away from here as you can." The little robot beeped and whizzed away across the sand. Soon he had disappeared entirely.

BB-8 and the map were safe . . . but Poe was not.

The battle was brief but brutal. Poe was captured by the First Order and taken back to their Star Destroyer.

As Poe was walked to his cell, one particular First Order trooper watched him go. This trooper was different. He didn't want to fight for the First Order. FN-2187 just wanted to be free. But he had no way to get away from the First Order.

As FN-2187 watched the Resistance pilot being shoved into his cell, a daring idea came to him.

Meanwhile, Poe was in great danger. He'd been captured by the First Order, and his mind was being probed by Kylo Ren himself. The dark side of the Force was strong with Kylo Ren, and even a man as stubborn as Poe Dameron didn't stand a chance against him. Before long, Kylo Ren had the information he needed about the map.

"It's in a droid," Kylo Ren said triumphantly, striding out of the interrogation room. "A BB unit."

The First Order began looking for BB-8. If the Resistance didn't find the little droid first, the galaxy would be in grave danger!

FN-2187 was ready to act. All he needed was a pilot . . . and the First Order had brought one right to him! He would help Poe Dameron escape and hitch a ride.

Now FN-2187 just had to convince the Resistance pilot to escape *with* him.

FN-2187 escorted Poe Dameron from his cell.

"Listen carefully," he murmured. "You do exactly as I say and I can get you out of here."

Poe grinned. "We're gonna do this," he said.

FN-2187 liked him already.

FN-2187 and the pilot snuck into the Star Destroyer's hangar and climbed into a TIE fighter.

The pilot was excited.

"I always wanted to fly one of these things!" he told FN-2187. "Can you shoot?"

FN-2187 had shot a blaster before, but he'd never used a ship's weapons. As Poe piloted the ship toward the hangar opening, the First Order troopers began to fire on them.

FN-2187 fired back.

He was getting the hang of it!

Soon Poe and FN-2187 were rocketing into space. The Star Destroyer shot its cannons after them.

"We have to take out as many cannons as we can," Poe yelled to FN-2187. "Or we're not going to get very far!"

FN-2187 aimed carefully . . . and fired. A whole bank of cannons exploded!

"Yes!" FN-2187 yelled. "You see that?"

"I saw it!" Poe yelled, laughing. Their TIE fighter sped away from the Star Destroyer, into the safety of open space. They had escaped.

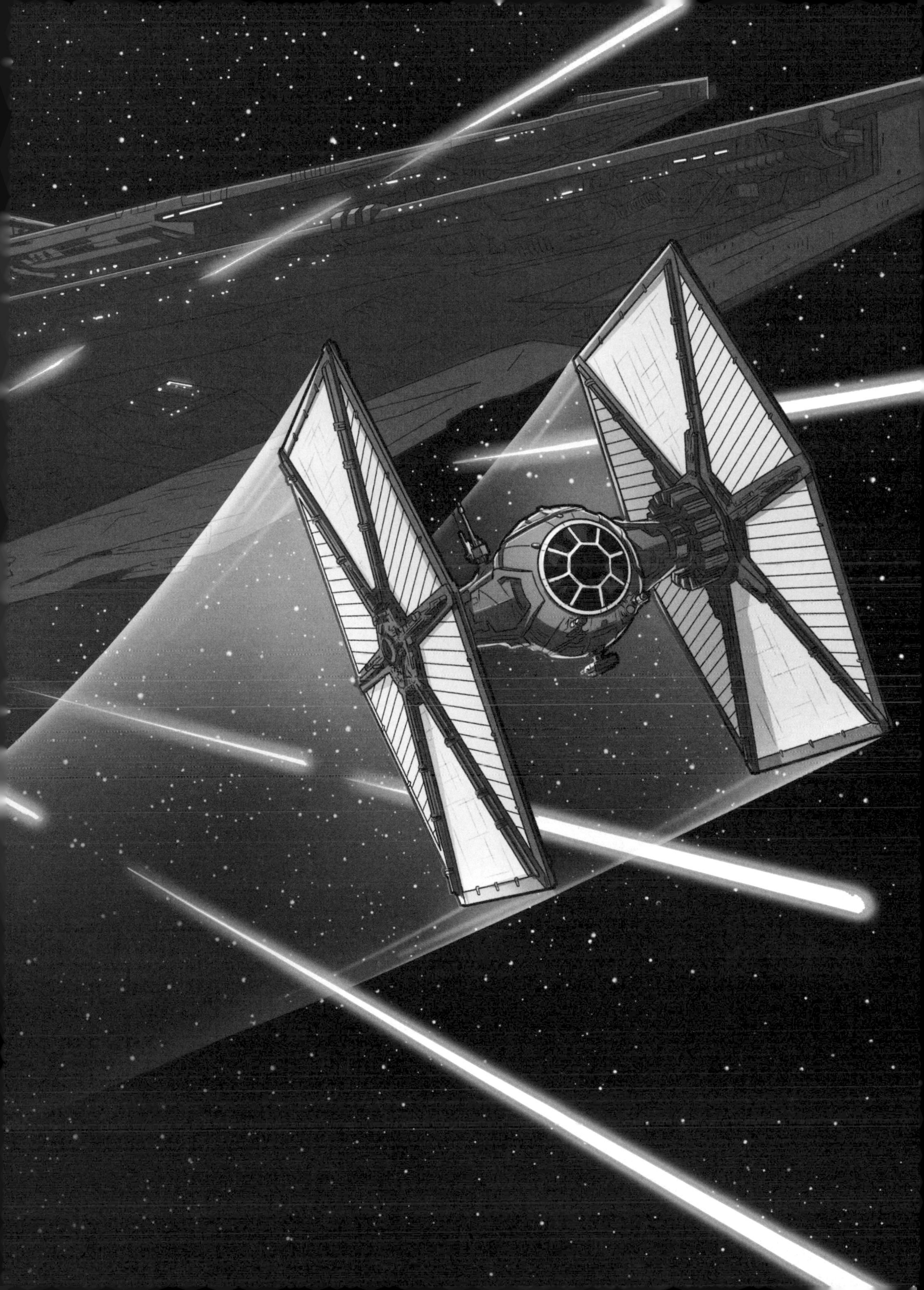

"Hey," Poe said to his new friend as he guided the TIE fighter through space. "What's your name?"

"Eff-Enn-Two-One-Eight-Seven!" the young trooper answered. Poe blinked, surprised.

"That's the only name they ever gave me!" FN-2187 explained.

"Well, I ain't using it," Poe said indignantly. "I'm gonna call you Finn."

"I like that!" Finn said.

Finn and Poe had escaped from the First Order. Now they needed to find BB-8 and get that map back to the Resistance. It was a tall order . . . but they were ready for their next adventure!

MISSION TO MAZ

Rey was an orphan who lived on the desert planet Jakku. She had found the little droid BB-8 when he was separated from his master, Resistance pilot Poe Dameron. The two had become good friends. BB-8 had even shown Rey the map to Luke Skywalker that he was carrying for the Resistance. The First Order wanted the map, too, and had tried to capture BB-8. But Rey had fought off the First Order stormtroopers and promised BB-8 that she would help him get back to the Resistance.

Now Rey, BB-8, and their new friends Finn, Han Solo, and Chewbacca were zooming across the galaxy in the *Millennium Falcon* to visit Han's friend Maz, who lived in a giant castle on the lush planet Takodana. They hoped that the alien could help them get BB-8 back to the Resistance base.

Maz greeted Han and his friends with a smile and served them a big meal. When she heard they were protecting a map to Luke Skywalker, she urged them to keep fighting against the dark side. But Finn shook his head.

"There is no fight against the First Order! Not one we can win."

Finn knew the First Order was looking for them, and he wanted to run. When Maz pointed to two pirates who would take him to the Outer Rim, Finn decided to leave.

Rey jumped to her feet.

"Don't go," she begged her friend.

Finn asked her to leave with him, but Rey said no. She had promised to help BB-8 get back to the Resistance, and she wouldn't go back on her word. As Finn left Maz's castle, Rey felt something pull her toward a stone stairway.

Rey followed the stairs to a long corridor and into a dark room. She lifted the lid of a wooden box and saw a strange object. It was a lightsaber!

But when Rey touched the weapon, painful images suddenly filled her mind. Some were memories from her lonely past, but some were of people and places she had never seen before.

Rey dropped the lightsaber and stepped back. She was afraid.

Maz appeared and rushed to Rey's side.

"That lightsaber was Luke's," Maz said. "And his father's before him. And now it calls to you!"

Maz explained that the Force moved through and surrounded every living thing. She told Rey to take the lightsaber with her, but Rey was scared. She shook her head.

"I don't want any part of this," Rey said.

She turned and ran out of castle and deep into the forest.

But Finn had been right. There was an enemy spy at Maz's castle. She had alerted the First Order, and the castle was under attack!

Blasts filled the sky as large black TIE fighters swarmed overhead.

Finn saw the chaos and ran back to help his friends. When he realized Rey was missing, he knew he needed to find her. Maz handed him Luke's lightsaber.

"Take it!" Maz urged. "Find your friend."

Finn nodded. He, Han, and Chewie raced from the castle to find Rey, but stormtroopers blocked their path.

Finn had never used a lightsaber before, but he had been trained to fight when he was a stormtrooper. Finn swung the lightsaber, battling his way across the rubble.

Rey skidded to a stop in the forest when a creature in a black cape and a heavy mask marched out of the trees. It was the man from one of her visions—Kylo Ren!

Kylo Ren was a dark warrior for the First Order. He'd come to Takodana to steal BB-8's map. He knew that a girl had helped the droid escape, and he wanted Rey to tell him where he could find BB-8.

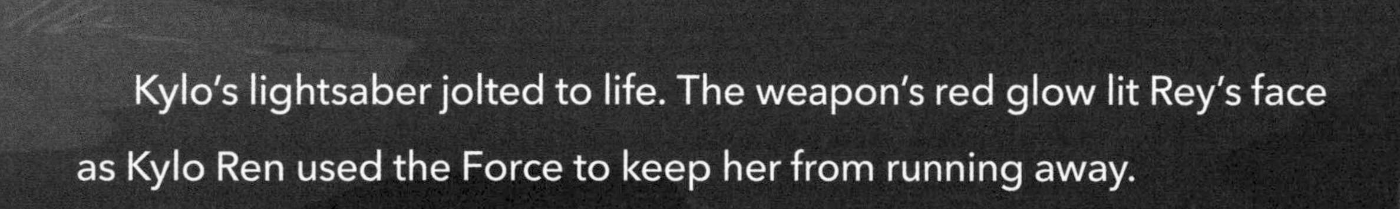

Kylo's lightsaber jolted to life. The weapon's red glow lit Rey's face as Kylo Ren used the Force to keep her from running away.

"The droid. Where is it?" he asked.

Rey refused to give up her friend's location, but Kylo Ren sensed that she had seen the map. He carried her back to his ship so he could ask her more questions. He was determined to find Luke Skywalker.

Just then, X-wings swooped in overhead, and the stormtroopers scattered.

Another spy in Maz's castle had alerted the Resistance! Poe Dameron and the Resistance pilots had come to the rescue, and they wasted no time fighting off the First Order from the sky.

But it was too late. Kylo Ren marched up the ramp to his ship with Rey in his arms. The black shuttle lifted off and shot through the sky, carrying Kylo and Rey all the way to the First Order headquarters—Starkiller Base!

As Kylo Ren's troops left Takodana, a new Resistance ship landed near the lake.

General Leia Organa walked off the transport and reunited with her old friends Han and Chewbacca.

But Leia's heart sank as she looked at the crumbled castle. She had spent her life fighting the dark side, and she was determined to protect her people from the First Order. She hoped using BB-8's map to find Luke Skywalker would help bring peace to the galaxy.

General Organa took Han, Chewie, Finn, and BB-8 back to her base. BB-8 and the map were safe, and the Resistance had a new mission: to save the galaxy by destroying Starkiller Base. But first they had to save Rey from Kylo Ren.

Rey had been a brave friend. She had helped return BB-8 to the Resistance. Now the Resistance would help her!

THE FIGHT IN THE FOREST

On the surface of Starkiller Base, an epic battle was raging. X-wing pilots fired blast after blast from their ships. Stormtroopers ran this way and that. It was total chaos!

The Resistance was fighting back against the First Order. And the Resistance was winning.

The First Order was an evil group of people trying to rule the galaxy. They planned to take over using their Starkiller: a powerful weapon inside a planet.

But the Resistance had figured out a way to blow up Starkiller Base's power reactor. Now the entire planet was cracking apart. Everyone needed to evacuate before it was too late.

Two members of the Resistance, Rey and Finn, were still on the planet's surface.

Finn used to be a First Order stormtrooper, but he no longer wanted to fight for the evil group.

Rey was an orphan who had recently discovered she could use the Force—a powerful energy field that could be controlled for good or evil. Rey used the Force for good.

The First Order had captured Rey and taken her to Starkiller Base as a prisoner. But Finn had rescued her, and together they had helped the Resistance blow up Starkiller Base's main reactor. Now they needed to escape.

"The ship is this way!" Finn cried as they ran through the snowy forest, back to the *Millennium Falcon*.

Suddenly, a dark figure blocked their path.

It was Kylo Ren! He was a dark warrior for the First Order. Kylo Ren could also use the Force. But unlike Rey, he used it for evil.

Kylo Ren was very angry that Rey and Finn had helped the Resistance.

"We're not done yet!" he shouted, igniting his red lightsaber.

Rey *hated* Kylo Ren. He had defeated her friend and his own father, Han Solo, during a confrontation on Starkiller Base. Han Solo was gone, and it was all Kylo Ren's fault.

"You're a monster!" Rey yelled at him.

That made Kylo Ren even angrier. He used the Force to slam Rey into a tree.

"Rey!" Finn cried. His friend had been knocked out.

Finn would have to fight Kylo Ren on his own.

Finn ignited Rey's blue lightsaber. It was a Jedi Knight's weapon, and he wasn't entirely sure how to use it. But he was going to try!

Kylo Ren sneered. Who did that traitor think he was to challenge Kylo Ren with the weapon of a Jedi?

"That lightsaber. It belongs to me," Kylo Ren said.

"Oh, yeah?" Finn replied angrily. "Come get it!"

Finn fought bravely. But Kylo Ren was very strong.

Crackle! Their lightsabers clashed against each other.

Sizzle! Finn's burning blue lightsaber grazed Kylo Ren's arm.

Kylo Ren howled in rage.

Kylo Ren slashed at Finn more powerfully than ever. Finn was caught off guard. He stumbled, and Kylo Ren landed a hit right in Finn's shoulder!

Then Kylo Ren swiped the lightsaber out of Finn's grasp and knocked him to the ground. Finn was badly hurt.

Kylo Ren turned off his lightsaber. The battle was finished. All he needed to do was take the blue lightsaber and escape the planet, leaving Rey and Finn behind.

Kylo Ren reached out with the Force. He commanded the blue lightsaber to come to him. But something was wrong.

The lightsaber flew to Rey instead!

Rey had woken up and used the Force to make the lightsaber come to her.

Now *she* would battle Kylo Ren.

Kylo Ren was shocked. How could a girl with no training in the ways of the Force overrule his command?

How powerful was she?

Kylo Ren intended to find out. He ignited his lightsaber again, ready to fight!

Rey battled furiously. But her swings were wild and off-balance. Kylo Ren backed her up to the edge of a cliff in the forest.

"You need a teacher!" Kylo Ren shouted angrily. He wanted Rey to join the dark side. "I can show you the ways of the Force."

"The Force," Rey whispered. She closed her eyes and concentrated. She felt the Force flow through her.

This time, when Rey used the lightsaber, her swings were strong and controlled. She pushed Kylo Ren back. She was going to win!

Suddenly, the ground between them split, opening a huge chasm. The planet was breaking apart. There was no more time to battle. If they didn't leave now, they would all be caught in the explosion.

Rey had to get back to Finn so they could get off the planet.

Rey sprinted to where her friend had collapsed.

"Finn!" she cried.

It was all right. Finn was just unconscious.

Meanwhile, stormtroopers arrived to help Kylo Ren. They picked him up out of the snow and carried him to a ship to flee the planet.

Chewbacca the Wookiee arrived in the *Millennium Falcon*. He had come to rescue Rey and Finn! Quickly, Chewie and Rey carried Finn aboard the ship. They only had seconds before the planet collapsed entirely.

KA-BOOM!

The First Order planet exploded in a fiery burst of light. From the flames flew the *Millennium Falcon*. The heroes had escaped, and the Resistance was victorious. The Starkiller was no more.

Rey was proud that she and Finn had helped the Resistance succeed. Still, she knew that Kylo Ren would be back. And if she was going to defeat him for good, she would need to train in the ways of the Force.

But first she would need to find Jedi Knight Luke Skywalker. . . .

POE'S PLAN

The Resistance had successfully destroyed the evil First Order's Starkiller Base, but the First Order had tracked the Resistance fleet back to their own base on the planet of D'Qar.

The last batch of Resistance troop transports was leaving the planet's surface to join the rest of the fleet in space. But they needed more time.

The First Order had arrived!

Ace pilot Poe Dameron looked to the leader of the Resistance, General Leia Organa.

He had an idea.

A crazy idea.

A crazy idea that Leia would surely dislike.

Leia knew all that without even hearing a word.

But they didn't have a choice.

They needed more time.

"Go," she told Poe.

General Hux of the First Order had been waiting for this moment with anticipation.

He wanted to put an end to the Resistance, and he had direct orders to do so from the First Order's Supreme Leader Snoke.

The First Order was going to demolish the Resistance base, destroy their transport ships, and defeat the Resistance fleet once and for all. But as Hux commanded his soldiers to prime the cannons on their ships, something shocking happened!

Poe Dameron and BB-8 zoomed toward the First Order Star Destroyers in Poe's black-and-orange X-wing. The tiny ship was dwarfed by the powerful fleet, and it confused the First Order officers.

With some help from BB-8, Poe was able to connect his comlink with the bridge of the Star Destroyer.

"Attention! This is Commander Poe Dameron of the Republic fleet. I have an urgent communiqué for General Hux."

"This is General Hux of the First Order," the officer barked back. "The Republic is no more, your 'fleet' are rebel scum and war criminals. Tell your precious princess there will be no terms, there will be no surrender."

"Hi," Poe replied as he continued to race toward the First Order fleet. "I'm holding for General Hux."

Hux was frustrated and confused. Poe and BB-8 stifled their laughs as he blathered on about the power of the First Order and how the Resistance was doomed.

"Okay, I'll hold," Poe replied.

He just needed to keep Hux distracted a little longer. . . .

Whoooosh!

Poe's X-wing booster engines flared to life and the fighter rocketed toward the First Order's massive Siege Dreadnought.

Poe dodged the First Order's clunky cannon fire and took out a series of surface cannons.

With some of the First Order cannons disabled, it was safer for the Resistance's bombers and the rest of the fleet to approach!

Poe had distracted the First Order long enough for the last of the Resistance transport ships to escape from the planet.

"Poe," Leia called over the comlink, "the evacuation is almost complete. Just keep them busy a little longer."

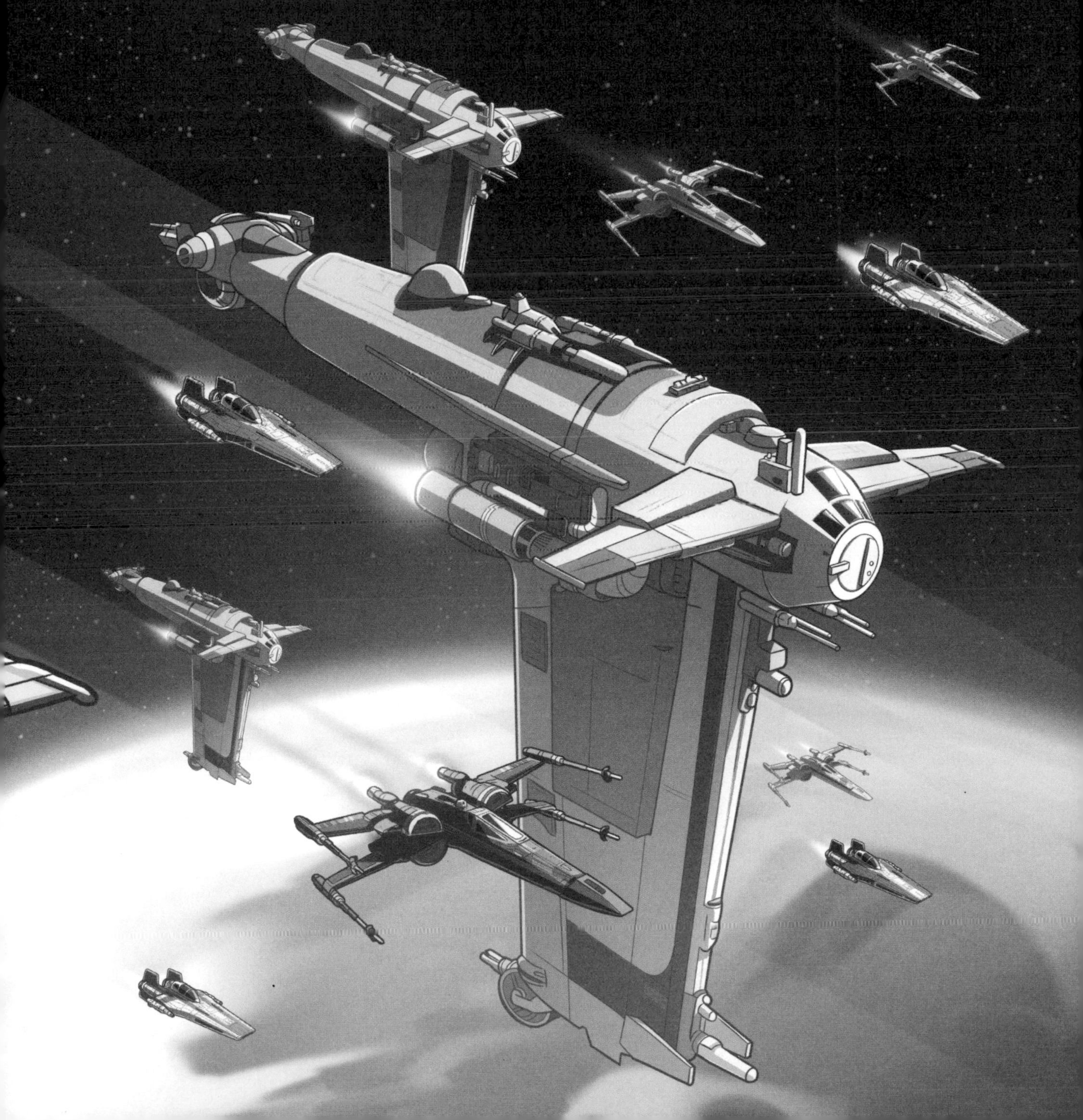

But before Poe could take out the last surface cannon on the Dreadnought, First Order TIE fighters screamed into battle. One of their blasts hit the underside of Poe's X-wing!

"My weapons systems are down, " Poe called to BB-8. "We need to take out that last cannon or our bombers are toast. Work your magic!"

BB-8 quickly got to work fixing Poe's X-wing while the battle raged on.

Infuriated by this new attack, the First Order's cannons started to fire at the surface of the planet below. The Resistance base was obliterated, but the last of the transports had connected with the fleet. The Resistance was safe, for the moment.

Poe knew they could destroy the First Order's Dreadnought. So rather than fall back and return to the safety of the fleet, he ignored Leia's orders and urged his squad to continue their space battle.

Poe was right, they could destroy the Dreadnought, and they did!

Many ships were lost, on both sides, but with the help of the bombers, the Resistance had struck a major blow to the First Order.

Poe and the remaining ships raced back to the Resistance fleet! This was their chance to escape so they could send out a call for help across the galaxy. If the Resistance was going to defeat the First Order once and for all, they would need all the support they could find!

CAPTURED IN CANTO BIGHT

The Resistance was in trouble. The First Order had found a way to track the Resistance fleet through hyperspace. With the First Order tracking them, the Resistance couldn't escape.

Finn and a fellow Resistance fighter, Rose, had flown to the glamorous city of Canto Bight on the planet of Cantonica. They were there to find the Master Codebreaker who could help them sneak on board the First Order ship that was tracking the Resistance fleet and disable the tracking device. But they had been captured by the Canto Bight police for crashing on a private beach and were locked in prison.

Time was running out. Finn and Rose needed to escape to help the Resistance!

Just then, a strange character inside Finn and Rose's prison cell roused. He called himself DJ, and he had been listening to Finn and Rose's troubles. He said he could help them.

Finn wasn't so sure. DJ didn't look like much of a codebreaker, but the thief promised he was well versed in the First Order's ever-changing coding system. For the right price, DJ said he could get them out of the prison cell and sneak them on board the First Order Star Destroyer.

As Rose and Finn decided what to do, BB-8 quietly rolled into the prison. He hadn't been captured, and he knew he needed to help save his friends. Good thing the police were preoccupied with a game of cards. . . .

Finn and Rose decided to trust DJ. They didn't have too many other options, and the Resistance needed them.

After DJ pressed a few buttons and smacked the cell door, it actually opened!

Finn and Rose were shocked.

But then they were *all* shocked to find that the three guards had been tied up by BB-8!

DJ applauded BB-8's handiwork. But there wasn't time for celebrating as more guards came running.

In all the chaos, Finn and Rose lost track of DJ and BB-8. They wanted to find their friends, but they needed to get away from the police before they were thrown back in prison.

Finn and Rose ended up in a stable. But it wasn't just any stable. It was a fathier stable. Fathiers were magnificent creatures, but the wealthy patrons of Canto Bight only wanted to watch them race one another around a track. The people didn't care about how the animals were treated. They just wanted to be entertained.

When the fathiers weren't racing, they were kept in stables, not unlike the prison Finn and Rose had just escaped.

Finn and Rose befriended the stable boy. He wanted to help the Resistance, too!

When the police reached the fathier stable, the stable boy pressed a button and all the stable doors suddenly opened, freeing the mighty fathiers!

The entire herd raced out of the stable, with Finn and Rose riding on the back of the lead fathier. The animals were fast! And they seemed to run even faster now that they were free.

The herd of fathiers raced around the track and then crashed through an intricate glass window into the grand hall of Canto Bight. Patrons scattered this way and that as the massive creatures crushed their finery underfoot.

Then the herd ran out into the streets, leaving a path of beautiful destruction in their wake as they trampled over sporty speeders.

But the police were following close behind. Finn and Rose needed to break away from the city!

Finn and Rose led the herd out to a sea cliff. The fathiers ran even faster in the wide-open space.

Rose noticed that the police were letting the rest of the herd go to focus their attention on Finn and Rose.

Suddenly, Finn and Rose's fathier slammed to a stop at the edge of a cliff, throwing Finn and Rose to the ground. Rose thanked the fathier. Then the animal ran away freely into the night.

Finn and Rose were trapped. The Canto Bight police would soon catch them, and all hope for the Resistance would be lost. But they had freed the fathiers. They had done the right thing.

Just then a sleek ship rose from behind the cliff in front of Finn and Rose. A hatch opened and BB-8 appeared!

DJ and BB-8 had come to the rescue. Rose and Finn jumped into the ship right as the police arrived! They had escaped!

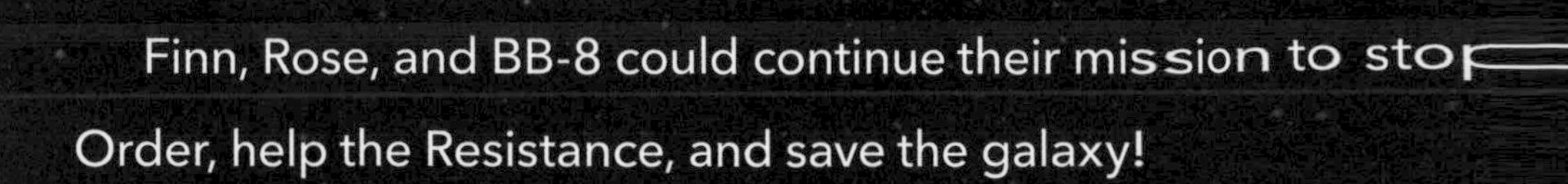

Finn, Rose, and BB-8 could continue their mission to sto

Order, help the Resistance, and save the galaxy!

Just then a sleek ship rose from behind the cliff in front of Finn and Rose. A hatch opened and BB-8 appeared!

DJ and BB-8 had come to the rescue. Rose and Finn jumped into the ship right as the police arrived! They had escaped!

Finn, Rose, and BB-8 could continue their mission t

Order, help the Resistance, and save the galaxy!

Just then a sleek ship rose from behind the cliff in front of Finn and Rose. A hatch opened and BB-8 appeared!

DJ and BB-8 had come to the rescue. Rose and Finn jumped into the ship right as the police arrived! They had escaped!

Finn, Rose, and BB-8 could continue their mission to stop the First Order, help the Resistance, and save the galaxy!